I Am Lavina Cumming

Also by Susan Lowell

The Three Little Javelinas
The Tortoise and the Jackrabbit
The Boy with Paper Wings
Little Red Cowboy Hat
The Bootmaker and the Elves
Cindy Ellen: A Wild Western Cinderella
Dusty Locks and the Three Bears

I Am
Lavina Cumming

A Western girl's Story —

Susan Lowell

Susan Lowell

Illustrations by Paul Mirocha

MILKWEED EDITIONS

First Published 1993 by Milkweed Editions
Printed in Canada
Cover design by Christian Fünfhausen
Cover photographs courtesy of the Minnesota Historical Society
Cover photograph colorized by Maranatha Wilson
Interior drawings by Paul Mirocha
Interior design by Ned Skubic
The text of this book is set in Palatino
08 09 5 4 3 2

Milkweed Editions, a nonprofit publisher, gratefully acknowledges sup-
port from Emilie and Henry Buchwald; Bush Foundation; Cargill Value
Investment; Timothy and Tara Clark Family Charitable Fund; DeL Corazón
Family Fund; Dougherty Family Foundation; Ecolab Foundation; Joe B.
Foster Family Foundation; General Mills Foundation; Jerome Foundation;
Kathleen Jones; Constance B. Kunin; D. K. Light; Chris and Ann Malecek;
McKnight Foundation; a grant from the Minnesota State Arts Board, through
an appropriation by the Minnesota State Legislature, a grant from the National
Endowment for the Arts, and private funders; Sheila C. Morgan; Laura Jane
Musser Fund; an award from the National Endowment for the Arts, which
believes that a great nation deserves great art; Navarre Corporation; Kate
and Stuart Nielsen; Outagamie Charitable Foundation; Qwest Foundation;
Debbie Reynolds; St. Paul Travelers Foundation; Ellen and Sheldon Sturgis;
Surdna Foundation; Target Foundation; Gertrude Sexton Thompson Charitable
Trust (George R. A. Johnson, Trustee); James R. Thorpe Foundation; Toro
Foundation; Weyerhaeuser Family Foundation; and Xcel Energy Foundation.

Library of Congress Cataloging-in-Publication Data
Lowell, Susan, 1950–
    I am Lavina Cumming / Susan Lowell ; illustrated by Paul Mirocha.
        p. cm.
    Summary: While staying with relatives in California after the death
of her mother, ten-year-old Lavina sees the arrival of the automobile
and experiences the great San Francisco earthquake.
    ISBN 978-1-571316-55-4 (pbk.)
    [1. California—Fiction. 2. Earthquakes—California—San Francisco—
Fiction.] I. Mirocha, Paul, ill. II. Title.
PZ7.L9648Iaac   1993
[Fic]—dc20   93-24155
                                                                CIP
                                                                AC

This book is printed on acid-free paper.

MINNESOTA
STATE ARTS BOARD

For Grandmama

With special thanks to my first audiences:
Mr. Stoner's fourth-grade class, 1989-90
and Mrs. Landau's fifth-grade class, 1990-91
(Rio Vista School, Tucson, Arizona).

Thanks for many kinds of valuable assistance are
also due to Douglas and Peggy Cumming, David
and Edith Lowell, Margaret L. Grade, and Ross,
Mary, Anna, and Melissa Humphreys.

I Am Lavina Cumming

I Am Lavina Cumming

CHAPTER ONE
The Ranch

 "I am Lavina Cumming, of the Bosque Ranch near Calabasas, Arizona Territory. I am ten years old. I am going to visit my aunt, Mrs. Agnes Scott, at 19 Vine Street in Santa Cruz, California. Please advise me how to get there."

Lavina watched her father write these words upon a card. His handwriting was decorated with loops and curlicues, surprisingly elegant coming from such thick rough fingers.

Father paused.

"Vine Street!" thought Lavina, imagining a jungle of terrible green creepers. "How will I ever find it, all by myself? What will they think of me? When can I come home?"

Lavina stared at the crease across Father's scalp where an Indian bullet had grazed the top of his head, long ago, before his hair turned gray. He dipped the pen once more into the inkwell and added that morning's date: "Saturday, September 16, 1905."

"Ouch!" said Lavina.

"Hold still," said Father.

He pinned the card to the shoulder of her best pink-and-white checked cotton dress.

"There," he said, and he stood back, studying her appearance with approval.

Yesterday, Lavina had heated two flatirons on the wood stove and ironed the dress herself, just as she had seen her mother do. And today she had boiled oatmeal for breakfast and washed up the bowls. She was the one who'd found the inkwell and the pen in Mama's old desk and brought them to Father.

"How will they manage without me?" she thought.

Stretching her neck until it hurt, she stared sideways at the card, but now the words were upside down, and blurry, and she couldn't read them anymore.

"Lavina of Vine Street," she said to herself. With the two long 'i' sounds, it almost rhymed. But it was not right. She was Lavina of the Bosque Ranch.

"Oh, Father!" she cried. "I don't want to go!"

"You must," her father said.

Under the stiff hat brim, his sunburned face looked tired and sad, but Lavina knew better than to argue with him. She squeezed back her tears.

"I love the ranch," she pleaded.

"I can't raise you here alone, Daughtie," Father said flatly. "Daughtie" was his pet name for her, short for "Daughter." Of his six children, she was the only girl.

"But I'm not alone!" said Lavina.

I Am Lavina Cumming

"I can handle the boys," Father said. "It doesn't matter so much if *they* grow up like savages."

Lavina had heard this before, and she knew what he was going to say next. Her temper flamed. She forgot to be obedient.

"But I don't *want* to be a lady!"

Father did not answer. Bending over to pick up her straw suitcase, he merely asked, "Are you ready, Daughtie?"

Lavina took one last look around the kitchen. There was the big black stove where her mother used to stand, before she died. There beside it was the wood box, where once, coiled up among the crooked black sticks of mesquite, Lavina had found a glittering cream-colored rattlesnake.

Lavina was not afraid of rattlesnakes. Careful is not the same as scared. Still, you don't want them in your house, so she and her next-oldest brother, John, killed it with a shovel. Then John took a knife, skinned the snake (which eerily continued to writhe), and hacked off a thick slice.

"John! What are you doing?"

The snake sizzled in the frying pan. John gave her a wicked grin.

"Mmm!" he said a few minutes later, chewing hard. "Take a bite. Dare, dare, and double dare!"

Although Lavina often regretted it afterward, she never could resist his dares, so she chewed and chewed and chewed.

"Well," she retorted at last, "it would probably taste fine if *I* cooked it."

"Come along, Daughtie," Father said.

Lavina had a new white straw hat with an elastic band that held it rather too tightly beneath her chin. She glanced into the hazy little mirror that hung over the washstand. A plump snub-nosed girl with hazel eyes looked back; her straight brown hair was already escaping from its thick braids. Her hat was crooked, so Lavina raised a hand and straightened it. But still she thought that the girl in the mirror must be a stranger, for she was all dressed up on a Saturday morning, and she looked frightened.

Father opened the door, and Lavina picked up her traveling basket. There was the big kitchen table where they all used to sit: Mama, Father, Tom, Bill, John, Lavina, Jim, and little Joe. There was the kerosene lamp that shed a warm golden pool of light at night but was black and sooty and hard to clean in the morning. There was the rocking chair in the corner, empty. Lavina set her front teeth into her lower lip, hard, and stepped out the door.

It was a brilliant blue morning, still early enough to be cool, especially in the shade of the giant cottonwood trees that surrounded the ranch house and gave the place its name. *Bosque* means "woods" in Spanish.

"Where are those boys?" Father grumbled.

Lavina's black mustang pony stuck his head over the fence and nickered softly at her.

"Good-bye, Chummy," she told him.

Chummy blew his grass-scented breath at her and nuzzled her pockets, where sometimes she kept a sugar lump or a carrot.

"Not today," she said, petting his velvety nose. She had not packed her boots and spurs and riding skirt. Father said she wouldn't need them in California.

Then they heard shouts. Down the dirt track that led to the corral rumbled an open wooden wagon driven by a tall boy of fifteen, Lavina's oldest brother, Tom. In the back of the wagon, four smaller boys bobbed and scrambled to keep their balance. Bill was thirteen, John was eleven, Jim was six, and Joe was five. All five brothers wore ragged overalls without shirts, and their tough dirty feet were bare.

"We've got a train to catch!" Father barked, heaving Lavina's suitcase in among the boys.

Quickly she clambered up a wagon wheel and spread out her skirt on the seat. As Father was taking his place, a distant high voice suddenly began to cry out, like a calling bird.

"It's Luz," said Tom.

A wrinkled brown woman no larger than a child, dressed all in black except for a purple scarf, emerged from the trees. Waving, she cried again in Spanish, "Wait!"

"What does she want?" asked Father impatiently.

"*Un regalito para Lavina*," cried Luz, running closer.

"She's brought me a present," Lavina said. She stretched out her hand, and Luz thrust a soft paper package into it. Heavy and warm to the touch, it smelled floury, delicious.

"Fresh tortillas!" said Lavina. "Oh, thank you. *Gracias*, Luz."

Luz raised one clawlike hand in a blessing.

"¡*Adiós!*"

"That's enough now," Father said. He clucked to the horses.

"¡*Adiós!* ¡*Adiós!*" shouted the boys in the back of the buckboard. "Good-bye!"

"Lucky!" called Jim to his sister.

"You ought to divvy them up with us," teased Bill.

"Naw!" said John. He switched to Spanish. "Who knows what that old witch put *in* those tortillas?"

"She is not a witch!" answered Lavina.

"Is too!"

"Prove it!"

"No speaking Spanish!" roared their father.

They were silenced. Since Father knew very little Spanish, he had forbidden his children to use it around him. But they had grown up speaking Spanish on the Bosque Ranch, and sometimes in the heat of the moment they forgot.

Luz lived alone down near the river. She had been their nurse and their mother's helper, and she did have a magical touch with flour tortillas. It was an art to stretch them thin yet not brittle, to make them tender but strong enough to wrap around a hot filling of beans or meat. She baked them on a sheet of iron (a flattened Standard Oil can, in fact) set over a little fire. And it was true that Luz practiced other arts as well. She knew what herbs would soothe a cough or settle an upset stomach—and perhaps she did dabble in good-luck charms.

I Am Lavina Cumming

"But that doesn't make her a witch," Lavina thought stubbornly.

Lavina looked back. The wagon moved slowly, but already the house was growing smaller, frailer, in spite of its walls of sun-dried adobe brick, two feet thick. High in these walls were windows made of small panes of glass, which did not admit much light, especially in summer, when the great cottonwood trees twinkled with leaves. Inside the shady ranch house the Cummings stayed fairly cool. Then when the cottonwoods lost their leaves, the extra light was welcome. And during the winter, the heavy adobe walls held the warmth of fires inside.

Lavina loved the house best when raindrops rattled on the corrugated iron roof like millions of dry beans. She loved to stand in the doorway and see the lightning flash against the San Cayetano Mountains, while the cottonwoods swayed in the whistling wet gray wind. Sometimes lightning struck the nearest hilltop. Sometimes she and John used to race out into the thunderstorms and run in the rain until they were muddy, soaked, breathless, and, after a blistering-hot day, cool at last.

Once, Father caught them and gave them both a spank.

"John did it first," Lavina said.

"Shut up!" retorted John, rubbing the seat of his dripping overalls.

"Don't *ever* let me hear you speak that way again," Father told John sternly. "No gentleman ever says that to a lady."

"I never intend to be a gentleman," John answered. "You need an education and money, which I don't have."

Father stood very still. The anger went out of his voice as he said, "You do not need those things. You need kindness, courtesy, and consideration for others."

"Well, anyway, she's no lady!" said John.

Lavina could feel her father's eyes upon her, so she did not open her mouth again. And finally, about a month ago, he sat down at the kitchen table and wrote a long letter to his sister, Mrs. Agnes Scott, in Santa Cruz, California.

Now the house looked like a toy among the trees. Luz seemed no larger than a black doll with a purple spot on her head. And then the trees were all that Lavina could see. Behind the Bosque rose the Cerro Prieto, a steep black hill that was hard to climb. But the view from the top was wonderful.

Lavina remembered how, before Mama died, the children used to sit under the giant cottonwoods in the late afternoon, listening to Father tell stories. He had lived in many places and done many strange and dangerous things. When he came out to the trees to tell Lavina and her brothers their evening story, he would ask, "What kind of story do you want?"

And they would always answer, "A true story!"

Sometimes Mama would interrupt his tales of Canada and California, of Indian wars and covered wagons and digging for gold. She held out a plateful

I Am Lavina Cumming

of slices of hot gingerbread and called, "Who wants gingerbread?"

The children would all run to her for a slice and carry one back to their father. And the story would go on.

All that Lavina could see behind her now was a cloud of pale brown dust. She bit her lip again to keep from crying and faced forward.

CHAPTER TWO
The Burro Train

At the tiny Calabasas train station, Father handed the reins to Tom.

"Come on, Daughtie."

Father planned to take Lavina as far as Tucson, the nearest city, where she would catch another train to California.

"Keep your ticket in your pocket," Father told her. "It's good practice for later."

Lavina stood upon the platform, feeling chilly. The tortillas made her basket heavier. Soon every well-known thing would disappear, and she would be on her own.

"What is California like?" she wondered.

She knew Calabasas well, for the village lay across the river from the Bosque Ranch, and the Cummings came here to collect their mail. In Spanish *calabasas* means "squashes," which grow in river bottoms, and sometimes Father jokingly called the place Squashville. Once, long ago, there was a Spanish mission at Calabasas.

Of course Indians lived there first, and the Cumming children found broken bits of their pottery everywhere and old dusty *metates*, or stones for grinding corn, just like the one Luz still used. Not long ago, while the railroad was being built, Calabasas had been a real town. But many buildings were abandoned now, their adobe walls melting back into the dirt.

Lavina looked at the San Cayetano Mountains, where she and her brothers often went exploring. The Arizona summer sky glowed a radiant blue, absolutely cloudless, above San Cayetano Peak. Sometimes, as darkness fell, the Cummings used to see pinpoints of light way up in the San Cayetanos.

"Indian campfires," her father would say.

And her parents would call the children in from play and bolt the door. They remembered fearful events, not long past. These Indians might be peaceful river or desert people, or they might be Apaches. To the west, a big canyon ran into the river. And just before Tom was born, something horrible had happened up that canyon. Lavina was still too young to hear all the details, but she could imagine them.

First, the quiet. Just as it was now . . . the singing birds, the children's voices. The morning sun. The cabin, roughly built of rocks and boards and canvas. And then the screams, the shots, the blood. And again the quiet.

"Your first Apache," old-timers warned, "may be your last."

The Apaches were members of Geronimo's band. The family was called Peck, and the father, stripped naked and left for dead, was the only survivor,

I Am Lavina Cumming

except for one young girl who was carried away as an Indian captive.

Someone touched Lavina's arm, and she jumped.

"Oh, Joe!" she said.

The bigger boys were off at a distance, throwing rocks at trees.

"I'm sorry you're going away," Joe said. "Can I have a tortilla?"

She looked down at him, and her heart softened. Immediately the others appeared, hands out.

"You buzzards," said Lavina, but she had no appetite now, either for fighting or for tortillas. She gave one to each brother and watched them eat. That left three for herself, later.

Father came out of the depot. "Almost time," he said.

"The burro's always late," mumbled John through a mouthful of tortilla.

Lavina's ticket was printed with the proper name of the train, "The International," followed by some highfalutin words in fancy type: "Daily Connections to Old Mexico via the Arizona and New Mexico Railroad." But actually the train was famous along its route for being as slow as a little donkey, so everyone called it the burro.

Suddenly there it was, first a glaring eye at the vanishing point of the track, and then a shriek! Lavina felt a great pounding in her chest beneath the pink-and-white checked dress.

"I'll be home tomorrow," Father told the boys. "Meanwhile, Tom is the boss."

He looked sternly at the four younger boys. "Do you hear?"

They became sober for a moment.

"Don't forget your chores," Father said. "Especially the milking."

They nodded. And then Bill shouted, "Look, it's the old diamond stack locomotive!" They all raced toward it.

"Stay off the track!" Father yelled.

The oldest engine on the line roared into sight. It wailed again, and then as it slowed and let off clouds of steam and smoke, Lavina thought it seemed to be sobbing. Flames leaped in the firebox. The boys hung back; they did *not* intend to be kissed.

"Don't forget to take care of Chummy," said Lavina to John. "You promised."

"Sure, Sis."

Now Father pushed Lavina toward the steps of the train, and she went, feeling like a prisoner. She leaned out the window, however, just as the burro puffed away, and she saw her brothers standing in a row by the wagon, waving. Then she remembered what her mother used to do, and she blew a rain of kisses over the boys, over Calabasas, and over the river, the ranch, the canyons, and the mountains, as the train pulled slowly from the station.

When she sat down, Lavina felt much better.

Clickety-clunkity, chickety-chunkety went the wheels over the rails. "Like someone dragging a heavy chain," Lavina thought.

She and her father sat side by side on seats covered with threadbare upholstery. At one end of the

I Am Lavina Cumming

carriage she saw a tall iron stove, to heat the car in winter, and at the opposite end a silvery tank that contained ice water in summer. When the conductor had punched their tickets, Father leaned back and pulled his hat over his face, but Lavina turned to the window with a bounce of excitement. Presently Father began to snore; Lavina had never felt more wide awake. The train zigzagged along Sonoita Creek until at last, no matter how she craned her neck, Lavina couldn't see San Cayetano Peak anymore.

Just past the tiny town of Patagonia, Father woke up.

"Now," he said, "you must watch for Pay-Car Curve."

"Why?"

"Well," he said, raising an eyebrow at her, "there's a story about that. Once upon a time, a railroad car carrying the payroll for a mine in Mexico jumped the track there and spilled bags and bags of money. They say some of it's still there. Here we go! Look hard! Do you see any gold and silver coins lying on the ground?"

Lavina scanned the ground until her eyes hurt. "No . . ."

All she saw was dry desert grass, which looked soft but really was not.

"Oh, well," said her father with a grin. "Maybe it's not a true story after all."

The train chugged along more slowly, climbing past distant, unfamiliar mountains, small mines, and here and there a settler's cabin. They crossed bridge after bridge, some of the trestles very high and rick-ety. Sonoita Creek glistened down below.

"This is the summit," Father said finally.

But this place did not seem high to Lavina. It couldn't compare with the view from the top of the hill behind the Bosque ranch house, she thought. Next the train stopped at a huge corral.

"We're going to load cattle," said Father.

The horses trotted about; the cowboys shouted and twirled their ropes.

"Oh, I wish I were out there!" thought Lavina.

At the Bosque Ranch the children helped Father work cattle. It was a hard, dusty job, but it was also exciting to see the large animals in motion, and to control them. Lavina and Chummy knew how to cut one cow out of a herd and how to guard a gap so that none escaped.

"This must be a huge ranch," she said. "Hundreds of cows."

Father nodded. Finally the cattle cars were hitched onto the train, and they moved forward again.

"Fairbank!" cried the conductor, walking down the aisle. "Connections to Tombstone!"

"Father," Lavina said, "if the money story isn't true, then tell me one that is."

"Hmm," said her father. He rubbed his rough chin thoughtfully and then began. "Only a few years ago, just exactly where we are right now, this very train was held up by robbers."

"Oh!" gasped Lavina, and Father went on with the tale. He used his special storytelling manner,

I Am Lavina Cumming

which meant that he would act out the different characters, and there would be surprises, and the children must sit very still. Any interruption would break the spell.

The Time They Robbed the Burro Train

It was a bitter February night in the year 1900. When the burro train made its usual stop at Fairbank, two masked men climbed into the engine, brandishing pistols.

"Stick 'em up!" they shouted. Everyone obeyed.

They forced the engineer and all the rest of the train crew to climb down and line up along the platform. Then three more masked bandits rushed to the car where Captain Jeff Milton, the Wells Fargo agent, was getting ready to throw off the baggage. He knew, and they knew, that the burro train was carrying many bags of money that night.

"Reach for the sky!" the robbers shouted.

One of them was the notorious outlaw called Three Finger Jack.

But Captain Milton did not obey. Instead he grabbed a shotgun and fired.

Three Finger Jack fell, crying, "I am shot; look out for that man!"

Jeff Milton had wounded him in the seat of his pants! The other robbers fired back, hitting Milton in the upper arm. He fell behind some large boxes, bleeding badly. Then the masked men began to fight among themselves.

"Now we're goners for sure!"

"Get the loot. Let's hightail it outta here!"

"I ain't goin' back in there."

"Do it, or you die!"

One outlaw forced another at gunpoint to climb back into the baggage car to rob it.

Suddenly shots rang out down the track! The gang of train robbers were frightened, and they headed for the hills. Two sheriffs' posses rode in pursuit of them, one from Nogales and one from Tombstone.

Captain Milton lay where he had fallen in the baggage car, on top of the money, in a pool of blood. But he was still alive.

"Quickly!" the engineer said. "All aboard! We'll back the train as far as Benson and get this hero to the hospital."

There the doctors wanted to amputate his wounded arm, but Captain Milton said, "Don't lay a hand on me, boys. Jefferson Davis Milton either lives or dies a two-armed man."

"And then?" asked Lavina.

"He got well," said Father. "He's fine today. Maybe his arm is a little crippled."

"Like yours," said Lavina.

The biceps of Father's left arm had been crippled by an arrowhead during his adventures among the Snake Indians in Idaho many years earlier.

"And the robbers?" she persisted. Lavina liked stories to have all their loose ends tied up.

Father looked down at her patiently. "One died,

I Am Lavina Cumming

Daughtie. One ran over the line to Mexico. And three were caught by the posses and went to prison in Yuma."

"Now," said Lavina, leaning against him, "tell me the story of the battle of the O.K. Corral." For the moment she'd forgotten all about California and the sad burden of becoming a lady.

"Oh, you know that one by heart," said her father.

"Please!"

"It's not much of a story," he answered gruffly, and she knew that this time it would be short. Still, she wanted to hear it once more. "It happened a long time ago, Daughtie, and the Earps and the Clantons were all bad men. Scum."

"But tell me about you. When you came driving in—"

"All right," he said. "Years and years before you were born, someone found a rich strike of silver in Tombstone. Overnight it became a town of seven thousand people, including me. I had a freighting business—"

Lavina forgot her manners and broke in. "This was *after* you went hunting for gold?"

"Don't interrupt," said her father with a frown.

She hushed. He went on. "And one day in 1881 I drove my wagon into the O.K. Corral—right into the middle of a gunfight between the Earps and the Clantons. Bullets went whistling up and down the street beside the corral. Nothing interesting about it, really. Scum!" he growled again.

"What did you do?" asked Lavina, although she really knew.

"My partner and I were unarmed. So we dropped to the ground, of course, and stayed put. We watched from behind the woodpile till the bullets stopped flying and the stupid fight was over. Then we unloaded our freight and went on with our business, like reasonable people. If fools kill each other, who cares? Guns are good servants, bad masters. Remember that, Daughtie."

"Where's Tombstone?" Lavina said. The afternoon was hot, and the rocking of the train made her feel sleepy. Her father's familiar shoulder was not too warm for comfort.

"Beyond those brown hills, over there," he said. "Now shut your eyes and don't ask any questions for awhile."

CHAPTER THREE
Sunset Limited

 "So many people!" thought Lavina, shyly following Father through the Tucson train station.

The hustle-bustle reminded her of the corral during a roundup, except that these were not cattle. She stared at boys in short pants (which her brothers thought were only for sissies) and at girls in starched, ruffled dresses prettier than her own. The other children all seemed to have mothers.

"Move along, Daughtie," said her father, and suddenly they reached the head of the ticket line.

A man looked up from beneath a green eyeshade. "Where to?"

Lavina listened with dread to her father's answer: "One way to Santa Cruz, California. And," he added, "this young lady is traveling alone. We need a through train so she won't have to change."

"Takes longer. Sunset Limited. Arrives Watson-ville tomorrow afternoon. Still have to change there."

"Someone will meet her in Watsonville," said Father.

With a sinking feeling in her stomach, Lavina watched her father's pile of dollars disappear. They were replaced by one very small ticket.

"We have time to eat," Father said.

Lavina had never seen a big restaurant before. She admired the white tablecloth, but she pitied the poor hot cook. "What a lot of dishes to wash!" she thought, and she asked bashfully for her favorite meal, chicken and dumplings. Her father sliced into a steak with gusto.

"Father," Lavina said. "Tell me again about Aunt Agnes."

"Well, we were born on a farm near Lake Ontario, far away in Canada," Father said. "The Cummings came to Canada from Scotland. There were eight of us children, four boys and four girls, and one by one all except the youngest daughter came West. I sailed around the Horn, following the Gold Rush to California. Our father was a harsh man to work for." He stopped for a moment and gazed at Lavina. "You are named for my mother, Lavina Nelson Cumming."

"And Aunt Agnes?"

"Agnes is older than I am. She was always my favorite sister."

Lavina tried to imagine an old lady with a face like her father's: broad cheekbones, piercing eyes, straight heavy brows, short gray beard. It was not easy.

"Will she like me?" she asked.

Father wiped his mouth and smiled at Lavina. "Aren't we all Cummings? If she likes me, Daughtie, she'll like you, too."

"Where will I sleep?"

"She has a big house in Santa Cruz," Father said. "Plenty of room. She lives there with her daughter Maude, Mrs. Temple; they are both widows. And Maude has a daughter about your age. They'll know how to raise a girl."

Lavina put her elbows on the table and leaned her chin on her hands. In spite of the chicken and dumplings inside it, her stomach felt hollow.

"It has to be this way, Daughtie," her father said. "Your mother was all alone in the world, you know. There's nobody from her side of the family who could help. And now it's time to go."

They walked back to the station through the heavy, hot air of the late afternoon. The horse-drawn streetcars and wagons threw up plumes of dust. As Father and Lavina passed a store of some kind with a swinging wooden door, the door burst open and a man came out, along with a rush of air. The air carried a smell like yeasty dough, but the store was dark inside. It was no bakery. Through the open doorway Lavina glimpsed one or two men's backs and the gleam of bottles.

"Come along!" exclaimed her father irritably.

Then she understood. She was not supposed to know, but she did. People had whispered; she had overheard things. This was a saloon, a place to drink whiskey and beer. It was the kind of place where her father went sometimes—even though her mother disapproved—and came home late. She had smelled that smell before. She looked anxiously around and realized that the street along the railroad track was lined with saloons.

She ran a few steps to catch up with Father, but all her words stuck in her throat. For there was her train, very much longer than the old burro, pulled by a shiny new locomotive, and carrying the words "Southern Pacific" in bright new paint on every car.

Father helped her find a window seat and settled her straw suitcase into the luggage rack over her head.

"I am Lavina Cumming," Lavina said to herself, "of the Bosque Ranch near Calabasas, Arizona Territory. I am not Lavina of Vine Street."

Father sat down in the empty seat opposite her.

"Now," he said. "Here is what you will do. You will ride all night and sleep in your seat. In the morning you'll be in Los Angeles. But you must stay on this train until it stops in Watsonville. Then you change for Santa Cruz."

He went on: "You may leave your seat to go to the rest room or to get a drink or to go to the dining car, but you will never get off the train till Watsonville. Promise me."

"I promise," said Lavina solemnly.

"Here's some money for your meals. Don't waste it on candy."

"I won't, Father."

"I'll send your Aunt Agnes a telegram to let her know when you're coming. Someone will be sure to

34 *I Am Lavina Cumming*

meet you. Don't forget to get off in Watsonville, or you'll end up in San Francisco."

"Father," said Lavina, "where's Watsonville?"

He laughed. "Sorry, Daughtie. Look, I'll show you."

So he drew a little map.

"Here's Arizona. Here's California. And these are the railroad tracks between them. See?"

"Does that help?"

"Yes," said Lavina, and she held the map so tightly that it crumpled.

The car was filling up now.

"What's the Cumming family motto?" asked Father.

"'Courage!'" answered Lavina.

Among Father's books was a small thin volume

entitled *The Clans of Scotland*, and sometimes he showed the children the entry under "Cumming." First came a family history, including the tale of an ancient Cumming who, in the heat of battle, bit off his enemy's nose. Lavina's brothers especially liked that part. Then there was a picture that Father called a coat of arms. "A warrior would paint it on his shield," he said, "to tell the world who he was." At the bottom of the coat of arms, written on a little curly scroll, was the Cumming motto—the single word "Courage."

Father leaned forward and patted Lavina's hand.

"'A coward dies a thousand deaths,'" he said. He was quoting from the fat volume of poetry that stood on the bookshelf at home. On the table beside his bed, Father always kept a Bible and a copy of Plutarch's *Lives,* a book about famous Greeks and Romans.

Lavina looked at Father and thought about the time a cannon full of gunpowder had blown up beside him, burning him all over. She remembered the O.K. Corral. She thought of the two old bullets buried somewhere inside him as he sat across from her. And she remembered how he worked all day on the ranch and still told the children stories after supper, or read to them from his books. She gave him a big smile, and when Lavina smiled, her hazel eyes sparkled and nobody looked brighter.

"That's my girl," said Father. He rose to his feet.

"All aboard!" called a voice in the distance.

"Write to us, Daughtie, and we'll answer your letters."

Lavina nodded. He kissed her good-bye and swung down the steps just as the train gave a few slow jerks and slid away from the Tucson station.

Soon the conductor arrived to punch Lavina's ticket.

"All by yourself, young lady?"

Heads turned, and Lavina felt quite important.

"I'm going to California," she said.

She leaned back against the plushy seat, noticing that this was a much fancier train than the old burro. They clattered toward the setting sun, and Lavina remembered the name of the train: "Sunset Limited. Now I understand!"

CHAPTER FOUR
The Necklace

 Several times in the night, Lavina woke just long enough to glimpse the muffled yellow lanterns of small depots in the desert. Then suddenly it was early morning: pale, cool, crisp, and new. The train rattled through a dry landscape that she did not recognize. Lavina rubbed her eyes, bewildered, for her head was still full of a dream.

She was back at the Bosque Ranch, following her mother through a field of little yellow sunflowers beside the riverbank. Lavina was tiny, and the flowers grew thicker and thicker, taller and taller, until she couldn't see Mama anymore.

Then she remembered everything. Her mother was gone. Lavina was on her way to California. Perhaps by now she was already there! And she was also very hungry. The other passengers in her car, all adults, were slumped in their seats, asleep.

"Don't they look silly with their mouths open?" Lavina thought. She wanted to giggle but knew she should not; grown-ups sometimes woke up cross.

"Well, at least you can get a drink of water," she said firmly to herself.

She filled the tin cup that dangled by a chain from the water cooler. The ice had melted overnight, and the water wasn't cool at all, but it refreshed her. In the washroom mirror she saw a familiar person— with smudged cheeks and pigtails like old frayed ropes. She did her best to rebraid her hair, wiped her face with the edge of a roller towel, and returned smiling to her seat. She had remembered Luz's tortillas.

They were delicious. And when Lavina lifted up the third one she found a surprise: a little bundle wrapped in a green corn husk. Whatever could it be? Hoping for more food, Lavina tugged at the thin strip of husk that tied it, and the gift tumbled into her lap.

It was a necklace.

Or rather, a magic charm. Luz had strung a collection of strange objects onto a cord. The first was a silvery religious medallion, an image of the Virgin Mary surrounded by rays of light. Then came a large clear glass bead, a blue jay feather, and a dozen bright red coral beans with dark spots on them that reminded Lavina of staring eyes.

She thought, "It's good that Father didn't see this. He wouldn't like it."

She chewed thoughtfully on the last tortilla. Sunlight poured in the train window and made the glass bead sparkle. The medallion glittered, and so did the blue jay feather. Lavina knew where a coral bean bush grew at home, and how the long pods twisted open in the fall, and that the pretty beans were deadly poison. Of course she also knew better than to eat them.

"I'll always keep this, to help me remember," she told herself.

When she had devoured the last tortilla crumbs, Lavina packed the necklace away. Soon the train left the empty desert behind, and she saw a few buildings, which gradually thickened into a bigger city than she had ever imagined, house after house, street after street. At last the train inched its way into the station at Los Angeles. Most of the other passengers got off, but here Lavina knew that she must wait.

She folded her hands and watched the people on the platform beneath her window. Her stomach growled. Father had mentioned the dining car, but she was too shy to ask the way. Inside the station she saw a sign that said "Restaurant." However, she knew that she must obey her father and stay on the train.

Beyond the passenger platform lay a freight-loading dock, and she watched a team of horses go clip-clopping by, pulling a huge open trailer. It was filled to the very top with round fruits, so bright in the midmorning sun that they seemed to glow all by themselves. Lavina's mouth fell open in astonishment.

"Oranges . . ." she breathed.

Sometimes in the winter, carloads of Mexican oranges passed through Calabasas on their way north and east, toward the rest of the United

States. But those trains did not stop. To the young Cummings, oranges were a rare treat: one apiece for each child as a Christmas present.

Then, as Lavina gazed at them, the oranges began to move. The driver miscalculated a turn, and the trailer tipped sideways. As it fell, the fruits rolled like marbles, spilled, and bowled by the thousands all over the freight dock, into the roadbed, across the tracks, under the waiting train, and onto the passenger platform, where travelers and railroad workers, adults and children, chased them wildly.

Passengers dashed from Lavina's train while she leaned out her window. She heard the laughter and cheers; she even smelled the fragrance of bruised citrus. In her hunger she could practically taste the sharp, sweet juice. But she had promised her father that she would not get off the train, and she kept her promise.

Later, a middle-aged woman sat down in the opposite seat, read the card pinned to Lavina's shoulder, and offered her an apple, which Lavina gratefully devoured. Finally a sandwich seller did pass down the aisle.

"This is a big adventure for you, Laveena," said the kind woman. She wore a pair of tiny spectacles pinched onto her nose in a way that looked painful.

"Yes, ma'am," Lavina answered politely. "My name is Lavina, ma'am."

"Oh! Well, Lavina, your aunt will be happy to see you safe and sound."

"Will she?" wondered Lavina anxiously.

The woman opened the *Ladies' Home Journal* and

caught Lavina staring. "Do you like to read?" she asked.

"Yes, ma'am. I finished all the school readers up through the sixth, and all the books in the house. But," she said frankly, "I didn't understand everything."

"Well, then," said the lady, "I'll read this magazine, and you read that one, and then we'll trade."

So Lavina read about the new short winter coats, and how to manage a hired girl, and how to polish silver, and why (according to the former president, Mr. Grover Cleveland) women should not vote. Meanwhile the train puffed along past lovely rounded golden hills. The sky was blue, but the sun was not as bright as in Arizona.

"I'm scared," Lavina said as they neared Watsonville, and then she covered her mouth. She'd forgotten the Cumming family motto!

"Good luck, dear," said the lady with the tiny spectacles.

"Are you ready, Sis?" asked the conductor, popping his head into Lavina's car. "Watsonville!"

The train slowed down, and Lavina anxiously studied the people waiting on the platform. There seemed to be no old lady with her father's face, in fact no old ladies at all. But she took her basket in one hand and her suitcase in the other and got off.

When her train steamed away, bell clanging, she stood there alone, feeling no bigger than a pin. Nobody came up to her. She waited. The train whistle died away in the distance. Nothing happened.

"Something is wrong," Lavina said aloud.

"I am Lavina Cumming," she told a porter who was carrying a large trunk along the platform. He shook his head and pointed toward the ticket office.

"'Please advise me how to get there,'" the ticket agent read from her card. "Hmm. What I would advise you to do, miss, is to catch the next streetcar to Santa Cruz."

And so she did, feeling smaller than a pin. But nobody met her there, either.

"So this is Santa Cruz," she thought. The city was built upon hillsides; tier upon tier of buildings rose above a wide curve of sand that marked the shore.

"Oh!" sighed Lavina.

That was the ocean, glistening, immense, and restless all the time, like a live creature, or like the river at home. But it was much bigger than the river or the mountains, bigger than anything she had ever seen, except the summer sky in Arizona. Lavina watched wave after wave gallop onto the beach and disappear.

"White horses," she thought.

She felt invisible, like a hole in the air. Was it all a terrible mistake? Didn't Aunt Agnes want her after all? She took a deep breath, making the card on her dress rise and then fall.

"I am going to live with my aunt, Mrs. Agnes Scott, at 19 Vine Street," she told the people on the streetcar.

"Get off here," someone said.

The sign read, "Vine Street."

And although Lavina herself felt small, her suitcase seemed to grow larger and heavier as she trudged up Vine Street, reading the street numbers as she went. Lavina stopped several times to rest and look around her. By now it was late on a lazy Sunday afternoon. The tall wooden houses on Vine Street were prettily painted and set behind front yards full of flowers, and to Lavina they looked like palaces in a fairy tale. She saw no vines at all. A few people stared curiously from their porch swings at the sight of a girl dragging a basket and a suitcase along the street.

She longed to go inside—somewhere.

"If this fails, what shall I do?" she wondered. She didn't have enough money to buy a ticket home. But perhaps even if Aunt Agnes didn't want her, she would help Lavina return to the Bosque Ranch.

But what if there *were* no Aunt Agnes? What if she were hopelessly lost?

"I am Lavina Cumming," she said to herself, "And I have courage."

At last she reached 19 Vine Street. The house was cream colored, and pink roses bloomed on either side of the door. She stumbled as she climbed the last step, tugging her suitcase along. She set her burdens down, took a deep breath, and rang the doorbell. Nothing happened. She waited and rang again. She leaned her weary head against the door.

"What now?" she thought.

And then she heard a faint sound inside: thump-step, thump-step, thump-step. And the doorknob turned, and the big front door swung open. A stout old lady stood there, leaning on a crutch. Beneath a lace cap her hair was white, and in her hazel eyes Lavina did see something of her own father.

"Are you Lavina?" she said.

"Yes, I am," said Lavina. "Are you Mrs. Scott?"

"I'm your Aunt Agnes, child. Thank heavens you're here! Come right in."

And she held the door wide open.

I Am Lavina Cumming

CHAPTER FIVE
19 Vine Street

 Lavina stepped over Aunt Agnes's threshold and into a new world. The ceiling of the Bosque ranch house was draped with unbleached muslin to catch the falling adobe dust. Aunt Agnes's ceiling was smooth white plaster, encircled by a flowery molding. The ranch house floor was made of bare planks, rather splintery, that creaked when you stepped on them. But here, waxed oak floorboards gleamed between rectangles of oriental carpet, and upon the wall there was a telephone, the first Lavina had ever seen in someone's home. Through an open doorway she could also see a parlor full of red velvet furniture, lace doilies, and little palm trees in brass pots. A canary bird sang in a fancy cage.

"We didn't know which train to meet," fussed her aunt. "I was worried about you, my dear."

At the end of the foyer, reflected in a mirror surrounded by a gleaming mahogany frame,

Lavina saw a bedraggled figure that did not fit into this setting.

"Father sent a telegram," she said in a small voice. Then she thought, "At least he said he would."

"It must have gone astray," said Aunt Agnes. "We haven't heard a word. But all's well that ends well!"

She kissed Lavina's cheek and stood back, observing her intently. Embarrassed, Lavina dropped her eyes to the flowered rug.

"Lavina was my mother's name," said Aunt Agnes softly.

Then she became brisk. "Come along, child. Let's get you settled in."

Lavina picked up her suitcase again.

"No, no. Leave that alone. The girl will get it," said Aunt Agnes from the foot of the stairs. "Bridget!" she called.

"Girl?" thought Lavina. Could this be her cousin, the girl about her own age?

A clatter came from the back of the house, a door creaked, and suddenly Lavina smelled food. Chicken, she thought. She felt dizzy with hunger.

"Yes, Mrs. Scott?"

It was a grown-up red-headed young woman in an apron—surely not her cousin.

"My niece Lavina has come. Carry her valise upstairs, please."

"Sure I will, ma'am. Poor lamb! All alone! You look a sight, you do."

Who was she? Then Lavina realized that Bridget must be a hired girl, like the ones she had read about in the *Ladies' Home Journal*.

Bridget seized the suitcase in one strong freckled hand and Lavina's basket in the other. In spite of her crutch and her stoutness, Aunt Agnes hopped up the stairs surprisingly quickly. Lavina's feet felt as heavy as two bricks. She had never been inside a two-story house before. They reached a landing decorated by a statue of a lady who daintily held up her marble robes with one hand and a small vase of fresh flowers with the other. Next they arrived on the second floor, and Aunt Agnes explained, "This is my bedroom, and the bathroom."

"Bathroom!" thought Lavina. She caught a glimpse of a huge white tub on claw feet, and a stained glass window. At home on the ranch, the Cummings took their baths in a tin tub on the kitchen floor. In warm weather they bathed outdoors in the cement tank beside the well.

"And," her aunt continued, "here's your cousin Maude's room, and, next, her daughter's room. She's little Agnes, after me, but we call her Aggie. They're at afternoon church, but they'll be home soon. Everyone's very eager to see you, especially Aggie."

"Sure, a playmate will do Aggie good, ma'am," put in Bridget.

"We've put *you* on the third floor."

"Three floors!" thought Lavina. "Just imagine!"

Aunt Agnes continued up a narrower flight of stairs, uncarpeted, but hung with four pictures in faded golden frames. Each showed a substantial strong-featured woman in a Romanesque robe, and each one was labeled at the bottom. First came Faith, her eyes rolled toward Heaven, and clasping a large anchor in her hands. Hope was next; she smiled vaguely under the arch of a rainbow. Then came Charity, dispensing small stony loaves of bread to a hunched-over multitude dressed in gray gowns. Finally, there was Love, crowned with roses, who sat upon a sort of throne and held several fat little angels tightly in her arms.

"I've moved meself to the room behind the kitchen, miss," said Bridget. "Very cozy it is, too. But you'll like the attic."

"That will do, Bridget," said Aunt Agnes firmly.

The room was painted white and contained an iron bedstead set on rollers, a washstand, and a small chest of drawers. The ceiling sloped at a sharp angle to the wooden floor, but still there was plenty of room to stand up. White curtains draped the large window, and through it Lavina could see the neighbors' roofs and tall brick chimneys, many treetops, and in the distance down the hill, the ocean.

"That's Monterey Bay," said her aunt. Then she pointed uphill. "In the afternoons, the fog rolls in."

And Lavina saw it coming, spreading out its fingers, cold and soft and gray, from the green mountains behind the town.

"Soon you'll feel at home," said Aunt Agnes. "Now let's unpack your things."

Bridget flung open the suitcase and revealed Lavina's little pile of clothes.

"Hmm," said Aunt Agnes. "Let's see. Yes, I believe that red dress will do for school tomorrow. Bridget, go see about supper."

"Oh, yes, ma'am," agreed Bridget. "Lavina must

be perished alive, and church always gives Aggie an appetite."

Footsteps came pounding up the stairs and a child's voice cried out, "Grandmama? Did she come?"

Aggie was a much smaller girl than Lavina. Her blond hair hung in long ringlets, her white dress was loaded with frills and ribbons, and she stared at her new cousin with round bright blue eyes. Under one arm she carried a large doll, also blond, with a china head and hands.

After a moment she pointed at the suitcase and said, "Is that *all* your clothes?"

"Hush, Aggie," said Aunt Agnes, but in a gentler tone than she had used with Bridget. "Say how-do-you-do to Lavina. She's tired after her long journey."

"Is she really going to live in Bridget's room?"

"She's going to stay with us and go to school with you. You'll be great chums."

Aggie spied Lavina's basket.

"Did you bring your toys?" she asked, and opened it.

She pulled out Lavina's comb and her best pair of hair ribbons and her toothbrush. Then Aggie found a crumpled piece of paper, still floury from the tortillas. Next she discovered the corn husk, and finally Luz's present.

"Ooh, what's *that*?"

She held up the necklace.

There was a short moment of silence. An odd look crossed Bridget's face. Aunt Agnes frowned. And Lavina wished passionately that she were back at home again. Even her brothers, even John in his most teasing mood, was better than this horrid brat, who in two minutes had made her feel ugly and poor, betrayed her secret, and—she felt sure—got her in trouble with her aunt. Silently the old lady took the necklace from Aggie and looked it over.

"Run away now, Aggie," said Aunt Agnes. "Lavina will come and play later."

Aggie moved slowly and regretfully toward the door, listening for all she was worth, but nobody said a word. Then they heard her run down the stairs and call, "Mama! Mama!"

Aunt Agnes turned to Lavina. "What is this?"

"Luz gave it to me. As I was leaving home this morning—yesterday, I mean."

"Luz?"

"She lives by the river. She cooks and does washing and—"

Aunt Agnes's face cleared. "I see. Well, you won't need it here in Santa Cruz."

Words of protest rose in Lavina's throat but she choked them back. She put out her hand for the necklace.

"Quite barbaric," said Aunt Agnes, as though to herself. "No, dear. This is not—. You see, we go to the Episcopal church, and you will, too, if you live in this house. You'll understand it all better when you are older. Here, Bridget, take this away and dispose of it in the kitchen. Now, Lavina, cleanliness is next to godliness. It's time for your bath."

Here there were no buckets to carry. Hot water

I Am Lavina Cumming

gushed from the faucet and filled the huge tub. Aunt Agnes unbuttoned Lavina's dress for her and unpinned Father's card from the shoulder.

"You won't be needing this either, my dear. What a miracle that you arrived in one piece. You're a very brave girl. I can't imagine what my brother was thinking of, not to let us know."

Lavina stood in a daze, feeling shy before this strange, decisive old woman, and embarrassed, too, by her own tattered petticoat.

No one had helped Lavina bathe since she was a little girl, when Mama used to do it. Aunt Agnes used scented soap, and the towels were snowy white. She washed Lavina's thick, incurably straight hair and combed out the tangles with a strong hand; Lavina's eyes filled with tears, but she never let them spill, or complained about the loss of Luz's necklace. To everything that her aunt said, she responded, "Yes, ma'am." Tiredness made her numb, as though the bath were cold, not warm.

In school Lavina used to love to spin her teacher's big globe and watch the foreign countries go whirling past, each a different irregular shape, each a different candy color, each labeled with a different curious name: Armenia, Borneo, Yucatan, New Zealand . . . She used to think that visiting them would be as simple as stopping the globe with a touch of her finger. Poof! Magically, painlessly, she was there. Everything around her might be different, but she, Lavina Cumming, would be the same. Now at the end of her first real journey, she was not so sure.

When the bath was over, they went downstairs to supper. Lavina was introduced to Aggie's mother, Cousin Maude, a quiet, willowy lady in a white shirtwaist and flowing skirt, with fluffy hair wandering away in wisps from the knot on top of her head. She wore a gold watch pinned to her shirtwaist, and a melancholy expression, and she placed an elaborate brass ear trumpet on the tablecloth beside her plate.

"Why, she must be deaf," thought Lavina.

But Cousin Maude rarely raised the little horn to her ear, except when Aggie said "Mama."

Under the warm gaslight, the plates were gold-rimmed china. The many spoons and forks were silver; Lavina sat tongue-tied, almost afraid to touch them. She had passed beyond being hungry, she thought, and into some strange, grim place where nobody ever ate—Iceland, she imagined, might be such a country—until the grand moment when Bridget bumped the swinging kitchen door open with her hip and bounced into the room, a steaming platter in her hands.

"Chicken and dumplings!" she announced.

Lavina's favorite meal, twice in two days! She discovered that she was hungry after all, but amid such elegance, how was she to eat? After saying grace, Aunt Agnes shot a shrewd glance over her spectacles.

"Begin with that fork, child," she advised.

Lavina found that the food made everything at Number 19 Vine Street seem friendlier, even Aggie. In the middle of supper the doorbell rang.

I Am Lavina Cumming

"Telegram, ma'am," said Bridget.

Cousin Maude raised her ear trumpet expectantly.

"From my brother Douglas, I suppose," said Aunt Agnes, tearing it open. "Aha! I see the problem. It was addressed to Number 19 *Wine* Street."

She and her daughter looked at each other with raised eyebrows. Loving thoughts of Father warmed Lavina's heart, just as the food had comforted her body.

"Of course he didn't forget me," she thought. "He never would."

"Wine! The idea!" said Aunt Agnes.

"Silly telegraph operator," murmured Cousin Maude. "You may be excused, girls. Tomorrow is a school day."

Lavina examined her room closely before she went to bed. She liked being high up. With the odd sloping ceiling and the big window, her room felt rather like one of the tree forts where she and John played some of their best games. And she liked being alone.

"What if I had to share with Aggie?" She grimaced at the thought.

There was a bright rag rug on the floor beside her bed, which was an old-fashioned iron affair with a brass knob on each of the four bedposts and springs that jingled when she sat down. Still, it seemed very comfortable. And she liked the framed picture on her wall. It showed a volcano in full flaming eruption against a turquoise sky, and at the foot of this black mountain, under a shower of cinders, little white human figures ran for their lives in all directions. Like ants when you stirred up their holes, thought Lavina. The label at the bottom read, "Mount Vesuvius."

Finally Lavina laid her head upon her pillow, and just as she began to feel homesick, she heard a little tap at her door.

It was Bridget, wearing a shawl over her night-gown.

"Whisht!" she whispered. "Not a word, now, dearie, but I saved this for you."

She held out Luz's necklace, the coral beans glowing crimson, the blue jay feather blue, the religious medallion shining, and the glass bead sparkling even in the faint light of her candle.

CHAPTER SIX
School

 Lavina sat up in bed and rubbed her eyes. Where was she? Then she saw Luz's necklace lying beside her white pillow.

"Oh, yes, this is Vine Street," she said to herself, "And today is my first day of school." Lavina's heart gave a lurch.

She buttoned up the red dress that Aunt Agnes had chosen, tucked the necklace in her pocket, and crept downstairs. The marble lady smiled on the landing, but all the bedroom doors were closed. A crackling noise came from the kitchen.

"Good mornin'!" said Bridget cheerfully, grinding coffee so fast that her right arm was a blur.

Lavina swallowed her shyness and said, "Thank you for saving—"

Bridget shook her head. "Not another word! Hide it well, mind you. That Aggie's a nosy young limb of Satan, and she'll be meddlin' amongst your things. She does with mine."

Lavina's hand flew automatically to her pocket.

Bridget slammed the lid onto the speckled coffeepot, a quizzical look on her face.

"Best wrap it in your handkerchief," she advised.

Luckily Lavina had one. She had ironed it herself, back at the Bosque Ranch—in another world, another time.

"That was *then*," she thought. "This is *now*. But I am the same. Aren't I?"

"What kind of stove is that?" she asked, blinking away a few sudden tears.

"Gas cooker," said Bridget. Briskly she stirred the oatmeal porridge. "No ashes. Ever so much cleaner than a wood stove. But you have to take care not to blow yourself to Kingdom Come."

A shrill scream came from upstairs. Lavina jumped in alarm.

"What's that?" It sounded like one of the piglets at the ranch.

Another shriek followed, but Bridget continued calmly with her work. When she had finished counting out the breakfast spoons, she said, " 'Tis only Miss Aggie having her hair combed. Good mornin' to ye, ma'am."

"Good morning," said Aunt Agnes, entering the kitchen. This time Lavina had not heard the thump of her crutch. "You're an early bird, Lavina. I hope you slept well."

"Yes, ma'am."

There was cream with the oatmeal, and fresh orange juice, and a basket of hot biscuits, but Lavina had lost her appetite.

"All ready for school, girls?" asked Cousin Maude, who breakfasted in a dressing gown.

"Of course." Aggie tossed her ringlets. Even dressed for school she seemed to wear a great many starched ruffles. "I'll show Lavina *exactly* what to do."

"That's my good girl," said her mother fondly.

"Don't speak with your mouth full, Aggie," said Aunt Agnes.

Aggie leaned across the table and grabbed the jam. She stared boldly at Lavina. "Have you ever been to school before?"

"Yes." Lavina felt her cheeks burn, and she longed to retort that she was good at school. But perhaps here in California the work was harder, and she would be sent down to the baby class. Under the table she slipped her hand into her pocket and fingered the necklace.

All too soon, Lavina thought, Aunt Agnes shooed the girls out the door. Cousin Maude lingered at the breakfast table, sipping her coffee from a flowered cup. Bridget had packed two lunches in dainty little baskets, each covered with a checked napkin. Lavina was used to taking her lunch to school in a five-pound lard pail, like her brothers and all the other children at their school. Just as the girls stepped down the porch steps, Aunt Agnes appeared at the door one last time.

"Do you have clean handkerchiefs?" she called.

They nodded, she waved, and they set off to school.

Aggie gave a skip that made her ringlets bounce like yellow springs. Lavina longed to touch one, to see if it was real. Or to pull one, to see if Aggie would shriek again.

"Actually," said Aggie, "I never take a handkerchief. I never need one."

Aggie had lied to her grandmother! Lavina was shocked. At the Bosque Ranch, lying was considered a terrible sin, but Aggie seemed unconcerned. They walked in silence until the Mission School came into sight.

"How big it is!" Lavina thought, and her heart fluttered again. What if she turned and ran away?

"So what was your old country school like?"

"Well," said Lavina, "it was called the Palo Parado School, and there were nineteen pupils."

Six of those nineteen were Cummings. She and John used to share a bench and do arithmetic from the same book.

"And one teacher? In one room?"

"Yes."

Brown-eyed, talkative Miss Pennington was Lavina's favorite of all her schoolteachers. She could be peppery if the children misbehaved, but Lavina vividly remembered the lessons that Miss Pennington had taught her, and especially the stories that she read aloud.

The best one was a fat blue book called *Juan and Juanita*, in which a young brother and sister were captured by Comanches in Texas. But the children escaped, along with their dog, Amigo. The Comanches chased them. Juan and Juanita hid. They

I Am Lavina Cumming

hunted, gathered berries, and survived many dangers, crossing the state of Texas on foot and alone, until at last they reached their home and their mother again. *Juan and Juanita* was a storybook, Miss Pennington said, yet somehow it all seemed true. Miss Pennington would miss her when school opened this year, Lavina thought.

"Did you have books and a blackboard and pencils and ink?" asked Aggie.

"Yes, of course," said Lavina impatiently. She forgot about running away and walked faster instead, so that Aggie had to hurry to keep up.

"And how did you get to school? Did you walk?"

"No, we rode our ponies."

"*Ponies!* Really?" Aggie's tone changed to envy. "*You* had your own pony?"

"Why, yes." Now it was Lavina's turn to stare. "We have lots of horses."

She thought of Chummy's funny long face, his soft nose, his big green teeth.

"Oh! Is it fun to ride a pony?"

"Yes." On summer days she and her brothers used to ride their horses through the countryside all day long. If they finished their chores first, and didn't get hurt or into trouble, and came home in time for supper, their father allowed them great freedom.

"Did you put the ponies in the livery stable while you were in school?" asked Aggie.

A livery stable at the Palo Parado School! Lavina laughed. "No, we hobbled them. They just grazed around the schoolhouse."

"Even though I'm only eight, I'm in the fourth grade," said Aggie. "I'm *pree*-cocious, everyone says so. I'm supposed to take you to Miss Hazlem's fifth grade, but she may place you in my class. *You're* probably backward, coming from Arizona. She *said*," Aggie continued ominously, "that she would *test* you first."

Lavina climbed the school steps beside her cousin, her heart pounding harder than it did when she and John raced their ponies along the riverbank.

Aggie waltzed boldly into the fifth-grade classroom ahead of Lavina. The sunny room was already full of pupils, more than the entire enrollment of the Palo Parado School, all strangers. The most important stranger was, of course, Miss Hazlem. She rose as they approached her big desk at the front.

"Good morning," she said.

Miss Hazlem was tall, neither young nor old, with a sweeping skirt and a crisp white shirtwaist. The collar rose high around her throat, and she wore a little bow tie at the front; a gold watch on a long looped chain was pinned at one side. Dark braids, as brown and glossy as carved wood, encircled the top of her head. She looked down at Lavina and smiled.

Aggie said, "Her name is—"

"I am Lavina Cumming," said Lavina.

"From Arizona," said Aggie. "She *says* she's finished fourth grade, but—"

"Thank you, Agnes. You may return to your own class now."

Miss Hazlem's voice was deep for a woman's, but musical. To Lavina's surprise and relief, Aggie closed

I Am Lavina Cumming

her mouth with an audible snap, as though she had shut a small purse, and marched out of the room without another word.

"Now, boys and girls," said Miss Hazlem, "you will finish the sums on the blackboard while I talk to Lavina."

Lavina stole a peek at the blackboard. "Well!" she thought. "It's just addition." She felt a glimmer of hope.

Miss Hazlem took her to a table at the back of the room.

"Now, Lavina," she said. "Do you know your multiplication tables?"

Lavina nodded. At least she *had* known them at the end of school. She hoped that she hadn't forgotten.

"Good. Can you say the twelves for me?"

Miss Pennington used to have her pupils sing their times tables to the tune of "Yankee Doodle," but Lavina could also recite them. She drew a deep breath and reeled them off at top speed, concluding in one triumphant burst: ". . . and twelvetimes-twelveisahundredan'forty-four!"

"Very good, thank you. We are still reviewing our arithmetic, as you see, but soon we'll go into long division, fractions, and decimals. Have you started them?"

"A little," Lavina said.

Miss Hazlem nodded. "Now, will you please read this poem aloud to me?"

She handed Lavina an open book.

"Life is real! Life is earnest!" read Lavina.

And the grave is not its goal. . . .
Lives of great men all remind us
We can make our lives sublime,
And, departing, leave behind us
Footprints on the sands of time.

"Very nice," said Miss Hazlem in some surprise. It happened to be one of Lavina's father's favorite poems; she could almost hear him rolling the words off his tongue.

"Can you speak any pieces?" asked the teacher. Lavina thought quickly. Then she began:

'Mid pleasures and palaces though we may
roam,
Be it ever so humble, there's no place like
home . . .
Home! home! sweet, sweet home!
There's no place like home, there's no place
like home.

She could not go on. She fumbled in her pocket for her handkerchief, and as she pulled it out, Luz's necklace tumbled to the floor. Lavina froze. Miss Hazlem, however, did not seem in the least perturbed. She bent over, retrieved the necklace, and handed it back to Lavina.

"Wipe your eyes, dear," she said softly. "Welcome to the class. You may take the desk at the end of this row."

CHAPTER SEVEN
Friends

 The girl who sat in front of Lavina was tall, with long droopy dark hair. She turned around, and Lavina saw that her eyes were dark, too, and her face seemed sad.

"Like a hound dog," thought Lavina.

But then the girl winked at her! In one second she went from sad to funny and back to sad again. Lavina was so surprised that she almost burst out laughing in spite of herself.

"Now, boys and girls," said Miss Hazlem. The strange girl turned away, and Lavina quickly straightened her own face. But her heart felt lighter.

"We have a new pupil today. Lavina has come all the way from Arizona Territory. Our congressmen in Washington are talking about combining Arizona and New Mexico into one big new state, but we shall see. Meanwhile, today we'll begin our American geography lesson with the original thirteen colonies. Who can name them?"

Hands shot up: "Massachusetts."

"New York."

"Virginia."

In Lavina's old one-room school, Miss Pennington called up small groups of children to recite at her desk while the rest worked by themselves. In Miss Hazlem's class everybody did the same lesson, and some of the subjects surprised Lavina.

In the window of the classroom, Miss Hazlem kept a large glass bowl full of water. It shimmered in the sunshine, and then Lavina saw something orange slithering and darting through it.

"Why, it's a fish, a live fish!" she thought.

Lavina had never heard of such a thing before. Miss Hazlem called the bowl an "aquarium," and the big glass jar of dirt and moss beside it was a "terrarium." A tiny real turtle lived there. It was amazing, Lavina thought, that at home on the ranch they worked so hard to keep the animals and dirt *out* of the house, and here they brought them in! But when the class got to grammar, she was on familiar ground, and she sailed through the lesson.

"The door has a *creak*," she wrote. "The *creek* is outdoors."

At recess the tall dark droopy girl came up to her, followed by a small round girl.

"Would you like to jump rope?" asked the dark girl in a somber tone. Lavina wondered if she'd just imagined the wink.

"Oh, yes," she said.

The little round girl produced a rope. "My name is Bertha Lee," she said. Everything about her was round, Lavina thought; her hair was cut as short as a cap. "Everybody calls me Birdie," she said, showing round dimples in her plump cheeks.

"I'm Susan Pitts," said the other girl sadly.

"She hates her name," explained Birdie. She and Lavina began to turn the rope. "She wants to be an actress, you see. Blue bells, cockle shells . . ."

Susan Pitts ran into the rope. Her long thin legs twinkled as she jumped.

"Actresses are not named Susan," she said. "They are called 'Sarah' or 'Lily.' Now, 'Lavina' might do."

"Oh, no!" said Lavina. "Not me!"

She had never seen a play, let alone an actress, and speaking pieces made her nervous.

"Look," cried Susan. "This is Sarah jumping."

She closed her eyes and went rubbery all over. Her skinny arms fluttered like tree branches in a high wind. Birdie and Lavina giggled.

"And this is Lily."

One hand went to her waist and the other to her hair. She fell into a slouch and sashayed past the rope.

"La—di—dah," she sang, very high.

Lavina laughed so hard that she dropped the jump rope. It wriggled away into the dust of the schoolyard, catching Susan's ankles, and Susan became Susan again.

"Another disgusting thing," she said tragically, "is *Pitts*."

"An actress cannot be named 'Pitts,'" explained Birdie.

"How do you know?" asked Lavina.

Susan merely rolled her dark eyes.

"Last summer Susan's parents took her to a play in the City," said Birdie, "and she hasn't been the same since."

"This city?" asked Lavina.

"Santa Cruz?" said Susan, shocked. "Oh, no. The City is San Francisco. It's a perfectly swell place."

"Your turn, Lavina," said Birdie. Lavina ran into the rope and they all chanted:

> Down by the seashore,
> Down by the sea,
> Johnny broke a bottle
> And he blamed it on me . . .

"What is Arizona like?" asked Susan.

"Well," said Lavina, trying not to miss a beat, "I live on a ranch with my father and five brothers."

"Are there wild Indians?" asked Birdie.

Lavina was about to say no when she remembered how Aggie had envied her pony. So she said: "Yes, and lots of horses and cattle, and rattlesnakes and mountain lions and sometimes a bear. And a witch."

"Oh!" The other girls were awestruck.

"Tell us everything," ordered Susan.

"She will," said Birdie in delicious anticipation. "She'll tell it to us, bit by bit, all year long."

Lavina tripped. "Oh, dear," she thought guiltily. "But it's almost all true!"

It was Birdie's turn to jump rope.

After a skip or two she said sympathetically,

"And now you have to live with Aggie."

"Awful Aggie," said Susan. "Nobody likes her. Those curls—that voice—" And she imitated Aggie: "Oh, Miss Hazlem, my *cousin* isn't a *bit* like *me*!"

"That's true," said Birdie, showing her dimples.

"Someday," said Susan thoughtfully, "someday Miss Aggie will get her comeuppance."

The rope whipped the ground with a steady, reassuring beat. "Awful Aggie"—that was good, Lavina thought. And what fun to have two new friends!

When Lavina and Aggie got home from school, Cousin Maude was playing a wistful, tinkling song on the piano that stood in the front room opposite the parlor. Lavina wondered if she would ever be allowed to touch one of the ivory keys.

"Maybe," she thought, "I can creep in sometime and do it when nobody's around."

She paused in fascination for a moment as Cousin Maude sang in a high voice: "Shine, little glowworm, glimmer . . . Lead us on to love . . ."

Then Lavina followed Aggie into the kitchen, where there were fresh sugar cookies. As Bridget passed the jar, she managed to whisper a mysterious message in Lavina's left ear: "BEDKNOBS."

"Whatever can that mean?" thought Lavina.

She couldn't find out because Aunt Agnes told the two girls to play together until supper.

"Take Lavina to your room, Aggie, and share your toys nicely," she said.

As with Father, there was no easy way to disobey, so Lavina followed Aggie's sulky back up the stairs.

Even her hair seemed to pout as she flung open the door to her bedroom.

"There!" she said. "If you break anything or don't put it *all back*, I'll tell."

The room seemed like a child's paradise to Lavina. There was a two-story dollhouse, complete in every detail: tiny dishes, beds, bathtub, even a piano with miniature paper keys. There was a multitude of dolls, big and little—dolls with pink wax heads and hands, china dolls, wooden dolls, and even a few rag dolls. They were all stylishly dressed, and most of them had golden curls.

Aggie gazed curiously at her cousin.

"Don't *you* have any dolls?" she asked.

"Yes, I do," said Lavina slowly. "But I left her at home."

Her old rag doll lay in the bottom bureau drawer at home. Her name was simply Dolly. Lavina hoped that the boys would leave her doll alone while she was gone, for Mama had made Dolly for Lavina many years ago, when Lavina was very little.

Once, when Mama called the children inside for lunch, Lavina accidentally left Dolly behind in the hay wagon, where she had been playing. By the time Lavina remembered her doll and came back for her, a cow had found her first and had eaten off one of Dolly's arms and all of her clothes. Poor Dolly! Lavina was terribly sad.

"Never mind," said Mama. "Come on, let's take a nap."

Lavina had cried herself to sleep.

However, she woke up to a marvelous surprise:

I Am Lavina Cumming

while she slept, Mama had sewed. She made new clothes and a whole new arm for Dolly, and embroidered an even more beautiful face than before. It was that face, with a smiling red mouth and dark, long-lashed eyes, that Dolly wore as she waited in the bottom drawer.

"Here," said Aggie, thrusting one of her shabbier dolls at Lavina. "You can have *her*. Let's pretend she's a cousin on a *short* visit."

"Let's take them on a trip to Timbuktu," suggested Lavina, recalling a name from Miss Pennington's globe. Aggie looked surprised.

"We-ell," she said. "All right."

And away they went, past pirates and sea monsters and doll-eating cannibals. Lavina would have tolerated worse behavior than Aggie's, just for the chance to touch her toys.

When Lavina went to bed that night, she remembered what Bridget had whispered to her, and she tested the brass knobs on her bed. They unscrewed! They were hollow! And inside, she discovered, there was room enough to store even a rather lumpy necklace.

CHAPTER EIGHT
Letters and Stories

 "Dear Father," Lavina wrote. Then she stopped and chewed her pencil, for she wasn't quite sure how to write a letter.

I arrived safely. Aunt Agnes is very kind to have me. Santa Cruz is a beautiful place. You can smell the ocean in the air, a little like fish. There is a hired girl here named Bridget, and Cousin Maude and Aggie. I go to the Mission School, and I am being a good girl, but I miss you all. Tell the boys hello for me. Please write.

Your loving daughter,
Lavina

Aunt Agnes gave her a two-cent stamp, and Lavina mailed the letter, but day after day passed and the postman did not bring an answer. Meanwhile, Lavina's new life settled into a routine. Santa Cruz became here and now to her, while Arizona faded. In school they read *The Song of Hiawatha*, by Henry Wadsworth Longfellow; Miss Hazlem's deep voice chanted the words aloud:

> By the shores of Gitche Gumee,
> By the shining Big-Sea-Water,
> Stood the wigwam of Nokomis
> Daughter of the Moon, Nokomis . . .

Miss Hazlem made the poem sound like music played on the lower keys of the piano in Aunt Agnes's parlor. While Cousin Maude practiced, Lavina often eavesdropped, sitting halfway up the stairs near the marble lady, whose white lips always wore the same elusive smile. She was about the height of a small child, and somehow in spite of her prim and chilly appearance, she seemed companionable. Then one day Aunt Agnes found Lavina there.

"Whatever are you doing, child?" she asked sharply.

Mortified, Lavina whispered, "Listening."

Aunt Agnes said nothing. Then she let her hand rest for an instant on top of Lavina's head.

Finally she said, "Well, someone might trip over you. Go on downstairs. Maudie won't mind. She likes an audience."

Aunt Agnes continued slowly upward; her crutch thumped on each step. From the third floor, Faith, Hope, Charity, and Love gazed serenely down upon the scene. And Lavina obeyed her aunt, because everybody in that house obeyed Aunt Agnes, almost always. It was her house—but that was not the real reason. There were moments when Aunt Agnes's nostrils flared and her eyes flashed in a way familiar to Lavina; like Father, Aunt Agnes expected to be obeyed. What if you didn't? There would be trouble, Lavina knew instinctively. So whenever she thought of the necklace hidden in the bedknob, her heart gave a little quiver of fear.

Cousin Maude had been considered "delicate" since her widowhood, and therefore Aunt Agnes excused her from most housekeeping and allowed her to take long naps on the sofa after lunch. How then, Lavina wondered, did Cousin Maude find the strength to spend hours playing the piano, and even to give music lessons to neighborhood children?

" 'Tisn't for the money," explained Bridget in an undertone. "Devil a cent that husband left her, but Mrs. Scott's got enough for everyone, or so I hear."

"Then why?" asked Lavina.

"It gives her a job, that's my guess. Takes her out of herself. Makes her think of something besides herself and that precious Aggie. But if she's deaf, how does she hear the music? That's what I'd like to know. Be off with you, now. I have to scrub my floor."

Cousin Maude's pupils ranged from foot-dragging six year olds all the way up to young ladies in long skirts, who wore their hair in puffy pompadours. But when Aggie received *her* piano lessons, Lavina didn't want to be there. *Plink, plonk, clunk* went the piano. And then Aggie would squawk.

"You have natural talent, Aggie," Cousin Maude would wail. "Why, oh, why won't you practice?"

When the other piano pupils came, after school or on Saturdays, carrying their sheet music in a roll, the lessons went more smoothly. Some students were learning long and fancy pieces, but the young ladies usually wanted to practice popular songs to play to their beaux.

One day soon after Lavina's arrival, Aunt Agnes's dressmaker came to the house and measured Lavina, to her great embarrassment, from her neck to her toes, chattering about fashion to Cousin Maude the whole time.

"Little jackets are quite the rage this winter, Mrs. Temple," she said. "Turn around, dearie. Suits and shirtwaists are still very stylish. And for evening, lots of lace and feathers . . ."

"Those new feather boas sound charming," murmured Cousin Maude.

Soon Lavina's clothes appeared, including a blue wool cape and a Sunday frock. Aunt Agnes took her to a milliner's shop to buy a new hat. There Lavina learned that "leghorn" meant a straw hat, not a type of white chicken as she had always thought. And Lavina's Arizona hat became second-best.

On Sundays the family always went to church, where Lavina was awed by the solemn service and amazed by Cousin Maude's singing. High trills and chirps spurted from her mouth; she sounded like Signor Caruso, the tiny canary in the cage downstairs, only much louder. But soon Lavina became accustomed to standing next to a soprano.

Usually Cousin Maude fed Aggie peppermints to keep her still during the sermon, while Lavina sat quietly and studied the stained glass windows and the congregation, especially the ladies' hats. The

I Am Lavina Cumming

brims flew up so sharply at both sides that Lavina was puzzled: how did the ladies ever keep them on their heads? With hatpins as long as daggers, she guessed, stabbed through their elaborate coiffures. (She had learned that Cousin Maude's pompadour was manufactured over a special little cushion called a rat.) Tucked under the sides of the hatbrims were the trimmings—flowers, fruits, ostrich plumes, and even the entire wings of birds.

Lavina's own new leghorn hat was decorated with pink, blue, and cream-colored ribbon. When she glanced at herself in the mirror, dressed for church, she hardly knew the girl who looked back. Surely this girl didn't know how to catch a horse and ride it bareback? *She* didn't fall in the mud while catching toads by the river, or hit her brothers with a stick. This girl minded her manners. When Aunt Agnes criticized her behavior ("Don't hold your knife like that, Lavina!") or her grammar ("'Doesn't,' not 'don't,' Lavina!"), this girl mildly replied, "Yes, ma'am."

And she always wore shoes. Lavina looked down with regret at her feet; she did miss going barefoot. But life in Aunt Agnes's house seemed to have changed the rest of her. This bashful girl dressed in white never flew into a rage. She looked, in fact, like a young lady.

Even Lavina's skin felt different—hard, like the marble lady on the staircase, as if she, too, were always cold. And her head felt different inside. She seemed to watch what happened from a long distance, without emotion, as though she drifted in a strange dream.

"I never imagined," said Lavina to herself, "that it would happen so quick." She blinked, and the lady-like girl blinked back. "Well, maybe I can go home soon," Lavina thought hopefully.

Aunt Agnes's house was not home: for one thing, Aggie was in it, too. And so school remained the best part of Lavina's new life. In arithmetic she enjoyed fractions. After long division, they seemed as light and frivolous as Cousin Maude's feather boa. And the class continued with the story of Hiawatha, whose magic mittens gave him the power to grind rocks to powder. When he wore his enchanted moccasins, each step he took was a mile long. He made himself a birchbark canoe without a paddle, "for his thoughts as paddles served him." The canoe traveled wherever he wished.

At recess Birdie asked, "Are the Indians in Arizona like Hiawatha?"

"No," said Lavina. "They're real."

She thought of the quiet canyon, the ruined stone house. The young captive girl on the back of the Indian horse. Or perhaps, thought Lavina, she walked. Was she ever rescued? Or did she escape? Father didn't know. Sometimes, he told Lavina, when they were finally rescued, captives didn't want to go home.

"My father knew a man who had an Apache friend," she said. "One day the Apache said to his friend: 'I'm going to disappear.' 'I don't believe it,' said the other. 'Turn your back and count to ten,' said the Apache. And he disappeared."

"No!" said Birdie.

"It's a story," said Susan. "Like Hiawatha."

"No," said Lavina. "It's true."

"But how?"

"They were standing on a grassy plain. No trees, no hills. The other man searched and searched but couldn't find hide nor hair of the Apache. Until . . . the Apache stood up! He was only ten feet away, lying very still in a crack in the earth with the grass pulled over himself."

Susan let out a whistle. "Great Caesar's green galloping ghost!" she exclaimed.

"What?" said Lavina.

"She learned that from her brother," Birdie told her. "He's fifteen. Her mother hates it. Isn't it wonderful?"

"I have a fifteen-year-old brother, too," said Lavina wistfully. "His name is Tom."

"Have you ever seen an Apache?" Birdie asked.

"No-o," said Lavina. "I don't think so. But there are other Indians, too, lots of them, all different." And she began another story, which Father often told to the Cumming children under the cottonwoods at home.

The Baby Twins

Once upon a time, my father lived in Idaho. The people there were called Snakes, because they lived along the Snake River. While he lived with them he sometimes ate dried grasshoppers, just as they did.

"Ooh!" cried Birdie, wrinkling up her chubby face.

"He said they were quite good," said Lavina.

"Go on!" said Susan.

"He also traveled down the Snake River, through many dangerous rapids, on a raft that he built himself."

"Did it paddle itself?" laughed Birdie.

"Well, it floated downstream," said Lavina. "He steered with a pole."

"Shh, Birdie!" said Susan impatiently. "Go on!"

And Lavina did.

But sometimes instead of peace, there was war. And once, after a battle, Father heard the sound of crying. He and another man looked all around and found two Indian babies—twins, a boy and a girl—wrapped in buckskin, hidden in a bush.

At first they didn't know what to do. They were two men, way out in the woods, alone, as far as they could tell, with two hungry babies. They felt afraid of the Indians but sorry for the little twins. So they waited for a while, but no one came back for the children. Then Father tucked one baby in one of his saddlebags and its twin in the other, and the two men rode back to the nearest settlement. Along the way they fed the babies hardtack biscuits and bits of jerky, and they gave them water from a spoon.

And when they got to town they took the little twins to the other man's mother. At first she

I Am Lavina Cumming

was very doubtful, but then she grew to love them and adopted them and brought them up. And the girl became a schoolteacher.

"And that's a true story," Lavina added.

The school bell had already rung for the end of recess, but the girls had barely noticed.

"We'll be tardy!" Birdie cried, and they all started to run.

"Look on the hall table," Aunt Agnes called when Lavina and Aggie got home from school one day.

There lay a letter addressed to "Miss Lavina Cumming" in Father's handsome handwriting.

"What does it say?" asked Aggie, pressing close.

"None of your business!" hissed Lavina.

Aggie looked startled, for Lavina had never used that tone with her before. "I'll tell," she said.

"Ladies and gentlemen never read other people's mail," answered Lavina stoutly. For a moment she felt almost like her old self again, and then she turned to her letter.

Dear Daughtie,

I am happy to hear of your safe arrival in Santa Cruz, and very sorry about the mistake in my telegram. You did fine on your own, as I expected. We are all well here at the ranch, and the crops are good this year. We miss you, Daughtie, but believe me when I assure you that this education will be the making of you.

Be a good girl and obey your aunt as though
she were

Your loving father,
Douglas Cumming

Lavina's eyes filled with tears, but before they could shame her in front of Aggie, she noticed a second letter inside the envelope.

"What's that?" said Aggie.

"It's from my brother."

Dear Sis,

Well I thoght I'd tell you the news around here. Miss. Pennington is awful sorry your not in school just us. I had to sit in the corner for putin a lizzard in Ermalindas lunch pail. Looks like a long year since I forgot the multiplcaton tables last sumer and alot of speling. Luz came and made us green corn tamales, real good too, she askd about you. Father caut me readin a dime novel called Diamond Dick the Daring Desperado he said it was trash and padled me and put the book in the stove too bad. Im takin good care of your horse dont worry. We won a race.

Your brother,
John

Aggie turned up her nose and marched toward the kitchen, her ringlets bobbing.

"I'm glad *I* don't have a stupid brother," she called over her shoulder.

I Am Lavina Cumming

Anger boiled up inside of Lavina. She and John sometimes fought like tigers, but she could never, never allow anyone else to insult him. Especially not Aggie. She opened her mouth to say something that she would regret later. But Aunt Agnes's voice came first:

"Aggie!"

"Yes, ma'am."

"I am glad that *I* have a brother," said Aunt Agnes. Thump-step, thump-step, she hobbled into the room. "Now apologize to your cousin."

"Sorry," mumbled Aggie.

"Birds in their little nests agree." Aunt Agnes's tone was stern. Her nostrils flared.

Thunderstruck, Lavina folded up her precious letters and slipped quietly upstairs. No matter how sweet her aunt might look, with her white hair and lace cap, if Aunt Agnes were a bird, thought Lavina, it would not be a soft silly dove or quail. It would be a hawk.

CHAPTER NINE
Halloween

 It was the night of October 31, 1905.

From the bay window in the parlor, where a carved pumpkin flickered, Lavina could see a huge bonfire at the bottom of Vine Street. Patches of fog curled through the darkness, mingling with the smoke and making the flames seem suddenly to fade away and then flare up again.

"Boys!" sniffed Aggie. "They always get in trouble on Halloween. But *we're* going to have a party."

Now Lavina saw a tall, thin shape and a short, round one appear out of the fog: Susan and Birdie. Aggie's friends came soon afterward, and Lavina's first Halloween party began.

Bobbing for apples, the girls squealed and splashed and soaked their dresses. Then they each put on a sheet for the Spook Parade, ending at the dining room table, which Cousin Maude had decorated. It looked like a picture in the *Ladies' Home Journal:* two pumpkins held glowing candles, and a third was hollowed into a fruit bowl and heaped with oranges and black grapes. They all feasted on Cousin Maude's special Lady Baltimore cake, three layers filled with fig-and-nut cream. And then they gathered around the fireplace to drink cocoa, crack nuts, and tell stories.

First it was Aunt Agnes's turn. Shivering enjoyably, Lavina was surprised to find that her aunt could tell a tale as well as Father did.

The Golden Arm

There once was a rich man who lost his arm. So he had an artificial arm made for himself from solid gold all the way down to the fingertips, which somehow—nobody knew exactly how—he could open and close, like this.

He wore it wherever he went, until one night while he was staying in an inn, the golden arm caught the eye of a robber. And while the one-armed man was asleep, the robber came into his room and stole the golden arm.

The one-armed man woke up and shouted, "Stop, thief!" And the robber shot him dead and ran away with the loot.

As soon as the robber thought he was safe, he sat down to catch his breath. He was just preparing to gloat over the prize he had stolen, when he heard a terrible voice roar out in the darkness:

"Who's got my golden arm?"

Terrified, he leaped up, seized the golden arm, and ran away again. Yet nothing seemed to be following him, so after a while he stopped.

I Am Lavina Cumming

"Who's—got—my—golden—arm?"

This time he ran until he was too tired to move. He fell down, and for a long time he lay as still as the golden arm. Then, slowly, the golden fingers began to open and close, open and close, like this.

"Who's . . . got . . . my . . . golden . . ."

Aunt Agnes's fingers reached out and pinched the nearest girl.

"Eeeek!" screamed Aggie.

"Really, Mother!" Cousin Maude stroked Aggie's curls. "She's so high-strung. You startled her."

"Then what happened?" demanded Lavina.

"Oh," said Aunt Agnes, knitting busily. "in the morning they found him there, stark raving mad. All he would say for the rest of his life was—"

"WHO'S GOT MY GOLDEN ARM?" shouted the girls.

"And—" She paused for a long moment. "Nobody ever found a trace of the golden arm."

Outside the cozy house it was a very black night, full of scampering noises and distant shouts.

"Boys!" said Aggie again.

"Last year I went out with my brother," said Susan.

"What did you do?" asked Lavina.

Susan winked. "I promised never to tell." Then she whispered in Lavina's ear, "It was swell. I dressed as a boy, and we soaped windows and rang doorbells and made booby traps and—"

"Do the goblin piece for us, Susan!" Birdie

interrupted. "That's a dandy one for Halloween."

They never had to ask her more than once. Susan sprang to her feet and opened her eyes wide. Aunt Agnes and Father still seemed like themselves when telling a story, but Susan changed herself somehow. First she was a young child: "Little Orphant Annie's come to our house to stay," she explained, "An' wash the cups an' saucers up, an' brush the crumbs away."

"I'm an orphan, too," thought Lavina. "At least, halfway. And so's Aggie, I suppose."

Then Susan became Little Orphant Annie, older, tougher, telling about the bad little boy who wouldn't say his prayers:

> His Mammy heerd him holler, an' his Daddy
> heerd him bawl,
> An' when they turned the kivvers down, he
> wuzn't there at
> all!

Then came the rude little girl who made fun of everyone: "She mocked 'em an' shocked 'em, an' said *she* didn't *care*!" It was an excellent imitation of Aggie's mosquito-like whine, and Lavina glanced around to see if anyone else had noticed, but all eyes were fixed on Susan.

She dropped her voice to a thrilling whisper:

> They wuz two great big Black Things
> a-standin' by her side,
> An' they snatched her through the ceilin'

I Am Lavina Cumming

'fore she knowed
                what she's about!
        An' the Gobble-uns'll git *you*
                    Ef you
                        Don't
                                Watch
                                        Out!

Everyone clapped, including Bridget, who leaned in the kitchen door. Aunt Agnes looked up from her knitting. "Come and join us, Bridget," she said.

"Tell us about Halloween in Ireland," said Lavina.

"Hallow Eve, we call it," answered Bridget in a faraway voice, as though she were remembering something sad. Suddenly Lavina thought, "Why, she must get homesick, too!"

"What happens on Hallow Eve?"

"We tell fortunes sometimes."

"How?"

"Ah," said Bridget, "if a girl steals a cabbage from a garden where she's never been before, in the moonlight on Hallow Eve, and if she takes that cabbage away, and she looks in a mirror in the dark while she eats it, she *may* see the face of her future husband."

"Did you?" asked Aggie.

Bridget only laughed and looked deep into the fire. After a moment she went on, " 'Tis a night when the spirits are abroad. Witches . . . now, I know a witch. A white witch she is, and she can magic a wart off your hand quick's you can say Jack Robinson. But on Hallow Eve you might meet . . . banshees."

"What's a banshee?" said one of the other girls.

"A fairy woman—an evil spirit. When the banshee screams, that means someone's going to die. There's a banshee on the island where I come from, in Bantry Bay in the west of Ireland. Not a soul will take the road through the wood where the banshee screams, not after dark, *especially* not on Hallow Eve."

"I know a story a little like that," said Lavina.

"Tell it!" said Susan and Birdie together.

And Lavina began the story that Luz used to call,

La Llorona

Once, just down the river from my house in Arizona, there lived a very beautiful girl, who was also so vain that she would never listen to good advice. She fell in love with a handsome bandit and married him, even though everyone warned her that he was bad. And they had two children, and then he ran away and left her and went back to a bandit's life. She was so full of sadness and hatred that she turned against the children and threw them into the river. Then she was sorry and ran along the river to save them and tripped and fell in, too, and all of them were swept away and drowned.

But that is not the end of the story.

She's still there. After dark, she haunts the river, dressed in white, still crying after her children. People call her *"La Llorona,"* the weeping woman. If you listen, you can hear her voice above the sound of the water. She wants children, any children. And bad children who don't come right home when it gets dark may hear her crying . . . and feel . . . something icy cold closing around their necks . . .

Outside, there was a wild scream and a crash. Everybody jumped, and Lavina broke off her story.

"Great Caesar's green galloping ghost!" said Susan.

"It's as black as Egypt out there," said Bridget, who had run to the window.

Now they heard the sound of sobbing.

"Go see what it is," said Aunt Agnes.

Bridget flung open the door, and there in the lamplight they all saw the figure of a small redheaded boy, pinned down upon Aunt Agnes's front porch by a large wooden ladder. In his right hand the boy clutched a piece of soap.

"Freddy!" gasped Cousin Maude.

Freddy was one of Cousin Maude's most reluctant music pupils. He much preferred teasing Aggie and Lavina to playing the piano. Once, while waiting his turn, he had inked a black mustache on one of Aggie's dolls.

"He was soaping our windows!" said Aggie. "He's a bad boy."

Bridget lifted away the ladder and helped Freddy to his feet, but when he tried to walk he cried out, "My ankle!"

"Bring him inside, Bridget," said Aunt Agnes. "You call his father, Maude."

Cousin Maude cranked up the telephone.

"Mr. Moberley?" she murmured into the receiver. "We have your Freddy here."

Stretched out upon the horsehair sofa, Freddy looked younger than Lavina remembered, and now she felt sorry for him. His freckles stood out sharply against his pale face, he was entirely surrounded by females, and his father was coming to get him.

"Just a sprain, I think, ma'am," said Bridget.

"Good," said Aunt Agnes. "Well, sir, what do you have to say for yourself?"

Freddy looked up at her. And suddenly he grinned.

"Trick or treat?" he said.

Freddy ate his Lady Baltimore cake on the sofa, while Mr. Moberley ate his in the dining room with Cousin Maude and Aunt Agnes. As Freddy boasted about his other Halloween adventures, and grumbled over being abandoned on Aunt Agnes's porch by his friends ("Those dirty rats," he said), Lavina caught snatches of the grown-up conversation. Aunt Agnes spoke very little; it was mostly the other two voices that Lavina overheard, and she never saw Cousin Maude use her ear trumpet once.

"Must apologize—at my wits' end since his mother died—"

"I *perfectly* understand—no harm done—sweet little boy—"

"Needs a woman's touch—lessons—delicious cake—"

I Am Lavina Cumming

Cousin Maude's laugh rippled lightly through the air.

"Good night, ladies."

"Good night!"

CHAPTER TEN
Rain

 One Saturday in late November, Lavina woke to a new sound. At first she thought it was wind sighing through the trees along Vine Street. But then she saw that the sky was gray outside, and it was raining, gently raining in a way that was strange to her. At home in the desert, rain was always a blessing, but mostly it came down with a crash and a bang in the summertime. This slow California autumn rain made her feel sad, lonely, trapped. She stood at the window in her nightgown and shivered. At home, she thought, the cottonwood trees would have lost their leaves by now.

Downstairs everything seemed more cheerful.

"Mornin'!" said Bridget. "A soft day, as we say in Ireland."

"Not a good day for picnics." Aunt Agnes unfolded her white napkin with a little snap.

"The piano will go out of tune," said Cousin Maude. "It always does when the rains start."

"Good!" said Aggie, eating jam.

"Silly girl," said her mother. "You still need to practice."

"Sit up straight, Lavina, and don't gobble," said Aunt Agnes, peering over the tops of her spectacles. "I can hear your teeth bite the spoon."

"Yes, ma'am."

"And that's enough biscuits, Aggie. You'll have dyspepsia, child. In my day, children ate only plain food, porridge or bread and milk, and they were the better for it."

"Nobody gets dyspepsia from hot biscuits any-more, Mother," said Cousin Maude, with her little laugh.

Lavina wondered what dyspepsia was. If it meant a stomachache, Aggie was more likely to get it from the amount of jam she ate. Then, as Aunt Agnes and Cousin Maude read the newspaper ("AIRSHIP SAILS OVER CENTRAL PARK"), Lavina watched Aggie stuff three more biscuits down the front of her white middy blouse. She caught Lavina watching and made a hideous face at her cousin. Blood sud-denly tingled in Lavina's ears. She heard a sound like the hiss of seawater as a wave hits the beach. She for-got to be careful. She made a hideous face back.

"Lavina!" exclaimed Cousin Maude in horror.

All innocence, Aggie bent her head over her plate. Her curls dangled dangerously above a sticky pud-dle of apricot jam.

Aunt Agnes laid down her newspaper. A picture of President Teddy Roosevelt grinned up at the ceiling, but nobody else at the breakfast table

I Am Lavina Cumming

was smiling. Aunt Agnes wore her most hawkish expression.

"We will not have these manners at table," she said icily. "Lavina, go to your room."

Lavina stood up. She felt hot and cold at once, and then she heard the blood rushing inside her ears again. She spoke back to her aunt.

"She started it," Lavina said, and pointed at Aggie. "She always does."

Aggie gave a little choke, while Cousin Maude began indignantly, "Really—!"

In the same freezing voice Aunt Agnes repeated, "Go to your room."

Lavina ran from the table and flew up the stairs. Her feet fell softly upon the carpeted steps as she passed the marble lady; then they pounded the bare wooden stairs, past Faith, Hope, Charity, and Love up to her own room and Mount Vesuvius.

"Oh, oh, oh!" she cried as she flung herself upon her bed and buried her face in the pillow. Tears soon washed away her anger, but then she felt very much afraid. What would they do to her?

"Outside—inside—everything's gray today," she thought.

She sat up and wiped her face with the back of her hand. "Good or bad, I am Lavina Cumming," she said aloud, and as she did so she felt her courage rise again, rather like her anger but steadier, not hot, but warm and solid as a rock in the sun.

"What's the worst thing they *can* do?" she asked herself. "Send me home? No, that would be the best thing they could do! What if they kept me, but always spoke to me sharply, like Aunt Agnes—or rudely, like Aggie? How could I bear it?"

As she sat there wondering, she heard a noise downstairs: not music, exactly, but melody under punishment. Aggie was practicing the piano.

"Now why would she do that?" said Lavina to herself.

She smoothed her hair away from her wet face and considered what to do next. Then the idea struck her.

"I know!" she said aloud.

Such a simple idea! Why hadn't she thought of it before? She took out her school tablet and pencil and started to write a letter home.

"Dear Father," she wrote, imagining his sun-burned face, shaded by the brim of his hat. But somehow Aunt Agnes's stern features intervened. "I hope that all is well at the Bosque Ranch."

She paused. How should she say it?

"I hate—" That looked too bad. She found a bit of india rubber and erased the words. "I can't—" Father didn't like to hear her say that. "Yes, you can," he would answer. So she erased again. "I want to come home," Lavina wrote. She underlined it hard.

But what would Father think? "Be brave," he was always saying to Lavina and her brothers. He had put each of them on horseback when they were two years old, long before they could reach the stirrups. If they fell off, he expected them to get right back on, and they always did. By the time Lavina was five, she helped to herd the cows on her own horse, just

I Am Lavina Cumming

like her brothers. She wore a divided riding skirt, and they wore overalls.

Still, she was a girl, "Daughtie." Lavina knew that some of the Cummings' neighbors, old women mostly, disapproved of the way that Father raised her. They gossiped that Lavina Cumming was running wild in the hills with her brothers.

"Old biddies!" thought Lavina bitterly. What did they know about it, anyway?

Now she studied the letter and added the word "please." She'd worn the paper awfully thin with all that erasing, she thought. Perhaps she should start over, on a fresh sheet, and work up gradually to the important part.

> Oh, Father, how big the ocean is! I waded into it and a freezing cold wave crashed over me. Salt water leaves you sticky when you dry. Then we sat under paper parasols and watched the people who come down from the City for vacations. The City is San Francisco, and maybe someday I will see it. Here on warm nights there are electric lights and music all along the pier.
>
> There are lots of horseless carriages in Santa Cruz. The automobiles smell bad and scare the horses. They go fast, but I don't think they could ever climb a hill like the rock-footed horses at home. Aunt Agnes doesn't have a carriage. When she wants to go somewhere she uses her telephone to call a cab.
>
> We went to see the redwood trees, which

grow up into the sky, much taller than cotton-woods. It's dark and cool in the forest and it smells like wet dirt and sawdust. The trunks are as big as houses, and my teacher Miss Hazlem said the trees are the oldest living things in the whole world.

It is raining here. Is it raining at the ranch?

She pictured the thunderclouds piled high over the San Cayetano Mountains, so white that they made the sky look bluer than blue, almost black, like Cousin Maude's sapphire ring.

How *was* she going to say it? She practiced the words in her head: "But I would rather eat dry jerky at home than roast turkey here. I'll never fit in. I'll always be the poor country cousin. Please let me come back."

Then she remembered something: she must ask Father for money. Every Sunday Aunt Agnes gave Lavina and Aggie each a nickel to put in the collection plate, and sometimes a penny for candy, but that was all. A ticket home would cost a great deal, and she knew that Father never had much money to spare.

Now Lavina felt absolutely desolate.

"I'm shipwrecked," she thought. "I'll have to take care of myself, like Robinson Crusoe."

Several ugly discords floated up the stairs.

"Except," thought Lavina, "I'd rather have canni-bals on my island than Aggie."

To comfort herself she unscrewed the knob on her bedpost and took out Luz's necklace. The coral beans, the glass bead, and the blue jay feather were

I Am Lavina Cumming

as bright as ever, but the little medallion had become rather tarnished. She polished it on a corner of her pillowcase, and as she did so, her thoughts wandered into the past.

Mama's voice was soft and low. She was teaching Lavina to knit, but the stitches puckered, the yarn snarled and shredded, whole rows came unraveled; Lavina wanted to throw the mess, needles and all, into the stove. But Mama repaired the damage and recited a little verse:

> If at first you don't succeed,
>   Try, try again.
> All that other folks can do,
> Why, with patience, should not you?
> Only keep this rule in view:
>   Try, try again.

Someone tapped lightly at Lavina's bedroom door, and in a panic she bundled the necklace beneath her pillow.

"Mrs. Scott says will you please come down." Bridget grinned at Lavina and lowered her voice. "When that Aggie got up from the breakfast table, three biscuits fell out of her underwear. Faith! What a hullabaloo! She's to practice her music for an hour, and you are to help stone the raisins. This is Fruitcake Day."

Aunt Agnes was at work in the kitchen, separating the seeds from a sticky black mass of raisins.

Lavina marched up to her and blurted out, "I'm sorry, Aunt Agnes."

"Very well, child," said her aunt. "Least said, soonest mended."

When at last this tedious work was done and the pans were filled, Bridget whisked them into the oven with a sigh of pleasure.

"Six lovely cakes! A good start on Christmas!"

"Christmas!" thought Lavina. Here was a new problem. At home on the ranch, the gifts were small and homemade, but there was something for everyone. Alone in California, with no money, what would she ever do about Christmas presents, especially for her father and brothers?

Aunt Agnes shook the flour from her apron and hung it up. The tart, spicy smell of baking fruitcake wafted from the oven, and Aggie poked her nose around the kitchen door. Suddenly Lavina had an inspiration, a "brain wave," as Susan would say.

"Aunt Agnes," Lavina said, "could we send one of the fruitcakes to Father and the boys?"

Her aunt turned around in surprise.

"It would be a Christmas present for them all," said Lavina anxiously.

Aunt Agnes smiled.

"A fine idea, my dear," she said.

CHAPTER ELEVEN
Christmas

 "There!" said Bridget when the last knot was tied on the fruitcake package. "And very nice it is, too. Although—" she whispered, " 'twould be even better with a spot of brandy in it, but don't you tell your aunt I said so, her being such a great teetotaler and all."

Lavina nodded. Aunt Agnes and Cousin Maude, in their best hats and gloves, regularly attended meetings of the Women's Christian Temperance Union, which opposed all sale and use of "intoxicating liquors." Carefully Lavina wrote upon the bricklike brown paper parcel:

> Mr. Douglas Cumming and Boys
> Bosque Ranch
> Calabasas, Arizona Territory

And Bridget went off to the post office to mail it.

At school they were practicing what Miss Hazlem called the "manual arts," cutting and sewing and gluing. For Father, Lavina glued a small calendar for 1906 onto a bit of decorated cardboard, and around it she lettered the words "Happy New Year." She wrote a message on the back: "Dear Father, think of me when you look at this. Where shall I spend the summer? Happy 1906 from your loving Daughtie."

The other manual arts project was a pincase made of chamois skin. It unfolded like a little book to reveal a row of shining straight pins; all ladies were supposed to need pins. When hers was finished, Lavina looked at it doubtfully.

"Aunt Agnes already has a pincushion," she thought, "and this'll never do for Aggie. It might be dangerous. She might stick them in *me*."

Bridget would like a pincase, Lavina decided. But what about the others? Luckily at this point Aunt Agnes gave Lavina and Aggie each one whole dollar to spend on Christmas presents, and Cousin Maude took them shopping. Lavina spent her money on new handkerchiefs for the two older ladies, and she also bought three fat candy canes: one for Susan, one for Birdie, and one—regretfully—for Aggie.

Lavina wrapped her presents in tissue paper and hid them in her bottom drawer. Even Aggie wasn't sneaky enough to open a wrapped present, she thought. And recently Aggie had been less annoying than usual, possibly trying to behave herself before Christmas.

The house on Vine Street was full of excitement. Mysterious objects were spirited out of sight when the girls got home from school. Bridget filled all the big crockery jars with cookies, and Cousin Maude made fudge, the most heavenly candy that Lavina had ever tasted. Then at school there was a Christmas program on the last day of classes, with holiday songs and scenes from Dickens' *A Christmas Carol*, and Lavina thought it must be as good as a play in the City.

Cousin Maude had invited Freddy Moberley and his father to Christmas dinner, much to Aggie's disgust.

"But he's a *terrible* boy, Mama," she pouted. "Every time he sees me he pulls my hair and shouts, 'Ding-dong!'"

"Now, darling, 'tis the season for peace on earth, good will towards men, remember? And," added Cousin Maude in a solemn tone, "remember that he has no mother to teach him how to behave."

"Yes, I know," agreed Aggie reluctantly. She submitted to a hug from Cousin Maude.

"Why," thought Lavina, "what's the matter? She looks scared. What could Aggie be afraid of?"

But this moment quickly passed, and in due time Christmas Eve arrived. Aunt Agnes herself mixed the plum pudding, which was wrapped in a cloth and set to boil all night, just like the one in Dickens. In the evening, as soon as darkness fell, Lavina and Aggie were sent upstairs, not as a punishment, but to wait for a great surprise.

"I know what it is, but I won't tell," said Aggie. "Here, you can play with this rag doll."

"Never mind," said Lavina. "I'll just look at your books. What's this? *The Wonderful Wizard of Oz*— what a funny name."

"I don't know," said Aggie indifferently. "I got it for my birthday."

"And you never read it?"

"It looked stupid."

"May I?"

"No!" Aggie snatched it back. "It's *mine*. Don't you want to know what the secret is? Have you ever seen a Christmas tree?"

"No," said Lavina. Certainly she had heard of Christmas trees, but the only trees at the Bosque Ranch were mesquites, hackberries, and cottonwoods.

"That's what Grandmama said. She said it would all be new to you. What *did* you do for Christmas? Did you even *have* Christmas?"

"Of course we did," said Lavina, stung. "We had turkey and stockings, and sometimes we had a *piñata*."

"What's that?"

"Well, a *piñata* is a clay pot covered with pretty paper and filled with candy and fruit. It's hung up high on a rope, and everyone is blindfolded and gets a turn to try to break it with a stick. There's a song you sing. *Dale, dale, dale . . .*"

They stood in a circle under the tree where the *piñata* hung: she, Tom, Bill, John, and some neighbor children. Jim was a toddler and Joe still a baby in Luz's arms. The *piñata* was shaped like a star with streamers dangling from each point, pink, yellow, blue. It was Bill's turn to be blindfolded. *"Dale, dale, dale . . ."* they sang, and he lifted the broomstick and swung it, hard. Candy rained down upon their heads, and nuts, and little oranges, the rarest of treats.

Aggie was staring at Lavina.

"I don't understand those words," Aggie said suspiciously.

"It's Spanish."

"Well, don't say it."

"Girls!" called Cousin Maude. "It's time!"

Downstairs all the gaslights were turned low. Cousin Maude flung open the parlor doors.

"Oh!" gasped Lavina.

In the corner of the parlor, a little fir tree twinkled all over with tiny candle flames. Among the dozens of candles hung red apples, walnuts painted gold, and artificial snowballs made of cotton. Aunt Agnes smiled from her favorite easy chair; Bridget stood beside the tree with a bucket of water handy.

"Merry Christmas!" everybody cried.

And underneath the tree were the presents, tied with ribbons. Aunt Agnes gave Lavina a blue serge skirt and a white middy blouse, just like Aggie's, and half a dozen new handkerchiefs. Cousin Maude gave her a whole box of fudge. And there was another box full of writing paper and envelopes, and a brand-new pencil, too.

Out of the corner of her eye, Lavina saw that Aggie also received school clothes, handkerchiefs, and fudge. Her mother had made her a frilly nightgown, and instead of stationery she got a pencil box. But two identical long packages remained under the tree. At last Aunt Agnes rose, slowly as usual, hobbled over to the Christmas tree, and handed one box to each girl.

Aggie tore into hers instantly, but Lavina stood still and simply held her gift in her hands. The package was quite light, with a heavier spot at one end and a large bow of pink satin baby ribbon. She hated to rip open such a perfect object; she wanted to let this moment sink into her memory forever.

"Go on, my dear," urged her aunt.

Aggie began to squeal. As she raced to show her present to her mother, Lavina caught a glimpse of yet another china doll with golden curls.

"Oh, well," she thought. "Maybe mine is shoes."

The box was about the right size, and hers were wearing out. She slipped off the pink ribbon and lifted the lid. A pair of clear green eyes looked up at her: she was the twin of Aggie's doll, except that her curls were brown. Aggie's doll was dressed in blue, and Lavina's in pink.

Lavina could not say a word. She picked the doll up and held her close, carefully cradling the china head. The doll's body was soft, and she smelled like new clothes.

Aunt Agnes said, "Ten is not too old for dolls. Is it?"

Lavina managed to shake her head. Everyone was looking at her, even Aggie, and Lavina hid her face in the doll's soft hair. Aunt Agnes took off her spectacles and polished them.

"Candles are burning low, ma'am," put in Bridget suddenly. "We'd best put them out now."

Then, in the gaslight, the rest of the presents were exchanged. Everyone seemed pleased with Lavina's gifts, and Aggie surprised her with a pair of red hair ribbons.

"Red is *your* color," Aggie informed her. "Mama says so. *Mine* is blue."

With her doll on her lap, Lavina could only smile.

After supper Aunt Agnes read " 'Twas the Night Before Christmas" aloud by the parlor fire. Then the girls hung stockings from their bedposts, and Lavina carefully tucked her doll into bed beside her. Santa Claus himself could bring nothing better, she thought as she closed her eyes. She wondered about Father and the boys at the ranch: what would their Christmas be like? She felt a pang at her heart, reached for the wonderful doll, and tumbled immediately into sleep.

CHAPTER TWELVE
Arabian Nights

 On Christmas morning Lavina's stocking was lumpy. And beside it lay a square, flat package—a book, she thought. She propped up the new doll to watch as she emptied the stocking into her lap.

An apple. Almonds. Round white candies with little red flowers in the center. A new collar edged in lace. Pink-and-yellow ribbon candy. Walnuts. A bag of jacks and a tiny red rubber ball. And, wedged in the toe, a glossy orange that left an oily perfume on Lavina's fingertips.

"We're rich!" she told the doll.

"But I can't call you 'Dolly.' You need your own special name. What? Oh, yes, you're right. I forgot to open the package."

The book was old, worn into curves at the corners. She lifted the dark red cover and read, in a formal handwriting much like Father's, "Agnes Cumming." Below that was written, in fresh ink, "To Lavina Cumming, Christmas 1905." Beneath that, the title of the book was printed: *Arabian Nights*. And below that she saw a small picture of a genie emerging from a lamp.

She turned the page and read:

> Once there was a magnificent and cruel Sultan of Persia who married a new wife every evening and beheaded her at sunrise the following morning, again and again, until the day on which he married a girl as wise as she was beautiful, named Scheherazade. Now Scheherazade, unlike all the other brides before her, had a plan.
>
> An hour before daybreak on the following morning, her younger sister knocked on the door (as Scheherazade had told her to do), and asked, "My dear sister, tell me I pray you, before the sun rises, one of your charming stories. It is the last time I shall have the privilege of hearing you."
>
> The Sultan gave permission. So Scheherazade began . . .

"Lavina! Lavina! Wake up! What did *you* get in *your* stocking?"

It was Aggie, her hair tangled and her mouth full of candy.

"I got a book, too, but *mine* has pretty pictures," Aggie said. "It's *Cinderella*."

After church, serious cooking began. Bridget was roasting a goose, and Aunt Agnes was making pies, and even Cousin Maude bustled around in an apron, taking an unusual interest in the hot and greasy parts of dinner. Lavina hid in the parlor and devoured

Scheherazade's tale of the merchant and the genie. Just as the genie poised his terrible curved scimitar over the merchant's neck and threatened to cut his head off, the sun came up! The rest of her story was even more wonderful, Scheherazade said, if only the sultan would allow her to live another day to tell it . . .

At this crucial moment Lavina had to hide her book. Freddy Moberley and his father knocked at the door, carrying a huge bouquet of flowers and an equally oversized box of chocolates. Mr. Moberley sported a fine long bristly mustache, and he smelled like cigar smoke, something of which Aunt Agnes disapproved almost as much as intoxicating liquor. But she welcomed him anyway, and Lavina stood by to enjoy the sight of a man and a boy again.

"Oh, really, Mr. Moberley, you shouldn't have," exclaimed Cousin Maude, accepting the flowers. Lavina noticed that she had taken off her apron and changed into her second-best lavender silk dress. "We are *so* delighted to have you and Freddy as our guests. Now, children," she went on, "you may each have *one* chocolate, so as not to spoil your dinners, and then run along and play nicely together."

"Well, he's not going *near* my dolls!" hissed Aggie.

Freddy looked ill at ease. In spite of his Little Lord Fauntleroy collar and short pants, which her brothers would despise, Lavina knew that he was no sissy. He reminded her of John.

"Let's go outside," she suggested.

There were some trees in Aunt Agnes's yard that

Lavina had wanted to climb ever since she came to Vine Street. Quick as a monkey, Freddy scampered up the tallest oak, and Lavina followed, picking her holds more cautiously since she was heavier, until she climbed high enough to look inside her room. She hadn't realized that the big brick chimney ran up the wall so close to her window, towering directly over the roof of her little attic bedroom.

"*I'm* not going to tear my dress," called Aggie from the ground. "*I'm* not going to get in trouble."

But Lavina knew that if you were careful, you didn't tear your dress, or get in trouble, either. She and Freddy landed safely at the bottom, dusted off their hands, and began to explore an interesting sheltered spot beneath a plum tree.

"This is a good fort," said Freddy, crawling in.

"I have a place like this at home," said Lavina. "It's where I keep my special rocks. Around it is my own country, Lavinalandia, with mountains and rivers and sultans and genies and slaves who turn into princesses. Sometimes I just sit there quietly, and the birds come and sing to me, and pack rats creep right up, and a Gila monster, too."

"What's that?"

"Oh—an animal, about so big, like a little alligator with a pretty beaded skin. If they bite you, you're dead."

"Golly!" said Freddy.

Aggie had tagged along, and stood outside the tree to listen.

"But my monster would never hurt me. I named her Esmeralda."

"What else do you have?"

"A big, brown, hairy, scary tarantula—a giant spider as big as a saucer, covered with fur."

"Hully gee!"

"Liar, liar, pants on fire!" cried Aggie.

Lavina solemnly crossed her heart. "It's all true. And my brother John has a fort, too. That's where he keeps his horses."

"Horses!" said Freddy. "How many?"

"Oh, seven or eight," said Lavina airily. "I can't remember all their names."

"His very own?"

Lavina nodded. She did not explain, however, that John's very own horses were a collection of special dry branches with curved ends. Every one did have a name, and John loved to groom and ride and talk to them.

"I have a horse myself. Chummy's his name, because he's so gentle. He's a black mustang pony."

"Gosh!" marveled Freddy. "We just have an old mare. But my dad says we might get an automobile soon."

"Really?" asked Aggie.

"Dinnertime!" cried Cousin Maude from the front door.

They brushed themselves off, but somehow Freddy had gotten very muddy. Fortunately the grownups were feeling indulgent that Christmas Day. Plates were filled and refilled with delicious things, from cream of tomato soup to slices of goose, which tasted like the dark meat of chicken, Lavina discovered. At last Bridget brought in the pudding, the pies (mince and cherry), and the fruitcake.

Then Lavina remembered her family in Arizona, and she felt another pang at her heart. She had heard nothing from Father or her brothers at Christmas. No letter, no card, no present. It was true that they never had many presents at the ranch, but still she felt neglected. Or could it be that something was wrong?

After dinner Mr. Moberley and the ladies drank tea, and Cousin Maude forced Aggie to play checkers with Freddy. Lavina slipped away into a parlor chair again and disappeared into the world of the *Arabian Nights*. Magicians turned people into cows, black dogs, and red deer; fishermen caught bottles full of genies; carpets flew; poor woodcutters discovered caves piled with gold and jewels; cut-off heads continued to speak; and Scheherazade saved her own head over and over again.

"She cheated!"

"Did not!"

"She moved that checker. I saw her."

"You moved it yourself."

"Let her win, son," said Mr. Moberley. "What does it matter?"

"Agnes," said Cousin Maude in an unfamiliar, firm voice. "Put the checker back and finish the game properly."

Lavina felt Aunt Agnes's eyes upon her, and she laid the book down guiltily. Until now her aunt had sipped her tea in silence across the room.

"Do you like it, Lavina?"

"Oh, yes, Aunt Agnes. It's wonderful."

"I have always liked it myself," said Aunt Agnes.

"I remember reading those stories for the first time in a dirty yellow book with very small type. Have you had a happy Christmas, my dear?"

Lavina nodded, but there was a lump in her throat. "Except—except I wonder how they are at home."

Aunt Agnes frowned. "But didn't you get your letter, child? It came yesterday."

Cousin Maude's hands flew to her mouth. "Oh, dear! I'm sorry, Mother. In all the excitement over the Christmas tree, I forgot to give it to Lavina. Now, where did I put it? Oh, yes. Here it is, on the piano."

In a flash Lavina had seized it. The thick brown envelope obviously contained more than just a letter.

"What is it?" clamored Aggie, abandoning the checker game.

Aunt Agnes said, "Go read it quietly in the dining room, dear. You stay here, Aggie, and defend yourself. I see that Freddy is about to jump every piece you have left."

Dear Daughtie,

I am sorry that this Christmas greeting comes so late. The rains have been very heavy here. When we went to Squashville last week to get the mail, Tom and I found an enormous flood coming down the Santa Cruz River.

Quickly we grabbed the package that you sent us, and hurried back to the ranch ahead of the water. We barely made it. We could hear it roaring towards us. In great haste we collected the other boys and loaded the wagon with hay, grain, groceries, and bedrolls—and the Christmas package. In the kitchen we had a box with a setting hen in it, so we lifted her, box and all, on top of the dish cupboard to escape the flood. Then we harnessed the horses and took to the hills.

We found a level little mesa top, where I sit writing at this moment. We've camped here for two days already, while we wait for the flood to go down. Now your brothers will each send you a Christmas greeting.

Tom wrote: "Sis, your fruitcake saved our lives. We've almost finished it." Bill added: "Your own Xmas present is down at the ranch, hope it's still dry." Jim scrawled: "Merry Christmas!"

John wrote next: "Im writtin now back home again after 3 days and 3 nights like old Noah or something. Guess what the setin hen hached out her chicks while we were gone gosh were they hungry and that ole hen was mad!!! We ate up the frutcake and all the crums. Thanks Sis. Chummy is fine you might want to know." In straggling letters across the bottom of the page was printed the word: "J-O-E."

And Father finished the letter:

I enclose a small remembrance for you, Daughtie, to remind you of home. Of course it was taken before the flood. The water marks on the walls show that the river ran a foot and a half deep throughout the house, but luckily my desk stayed dry. The well was flooded, too, so we shall boil our drinking water for some time

to come. I am happy to think of you safe and
comfortable with your aunt in California.

The Christmas present was a photograph. It
showed Father, Tom, Bill, Jim, John, and Joe, some of
them on horseback and some on foot, standing with
two or three dogs under the cottonwoods in front of
the Bosque ranch house. In the background there
was a small shadow; after staring at it hard, Lavina
felt almost certain that it was Luz.

CHAPTER THIRTEEN
Princess Perizade

 On rainy days, Lavina and Aggie walked to the Mission School beneath a shared umbrella, wrangling over who would hold the handle.

"I should, since I'm taller," argued Lavina, reasonably she felt, because otherwise she had to stoop.

"No, *I* should, 'cause it's *my* Grandmama's umbrella."

"She's my aunt. And besides, she told me to keep it during the day."

"I don't care. I want to hold it *now*."

Aggie made a grab at the umbrella, which wobbled, and chilly raindrops spilled down the backs of both their necks. Lavina tried to control her temper, but it was as hard as reining in one of the stubborn little brown burros on the Bosque Ranch. She wished she could close the umbrella and give Aggie a good poke with it. But young ladies did not do such things—and neither did girls who wanted to arrive at school dry.

In Miss Hazlem's class, while the wet wraps steamed in the cloakroom, Lavina learned about dictionaries, percentages, and the habits of wild beasts. Her class read from a history book called *How Our Grandfathers Lived*, and they wrote compositions and copied them over neatly, dipping their pens into the blue-black pools deep inside their inkwells. During indoor recess, Lavina and Susan and Birdie became expert at playing jacks. After school, Lavina and Aggie walked down Vine Street together again.

"You hold the bottom of the handle, Aggie, and I'll hold higher up."

"No."

They reached home more or less damp.

Every evening, Lavina told the story of the day to her doll, who was still nameless.

"Victoria?" she asked, as she curled up in bed one night in January. "Too old-fashioned, you say? Annabella? Too prissy. Valentina? No?"

The doll looked back at her with an intelligent expression. She was a true friend, who always understood what Lavina meant, even when she spoke Spanish for old times' sake.

"Today," Lavina said, "we studied Indians. We read a book called *Wigwam Stories*.

"And then Miss Hazlem asked us to write compositions. So I wrote the story of Father and the Apaches, a true story, you know. Do you want to hear it?"

And the doll did.

Father and the Apaches
By Lavina Cumming

Long ago, when my father used to drive freight wagons out of Tombstone, the Apaches were on the warpath all across the Territory. He camped one night far from town. As usual, he staked out his horses some distance from his wagon, spread his bedroll underneath the wagon, and fell asleep.

In the middle of the night, he woke suddenly. "Strange noises!" he thought, so he lay very still and listened carefully. His horses stamped and snorted, but those were familiar sounds to him. Except—it sounded like too many horses! Then he heard something else. A twig crackled. A man muttered in a strange language. And he said to himself: "Apaches!"

He lay stiller than ever as he considered what to do.

If he tried to escape on foot, they would certainly hear him, and they would probably catch and kill him. They must know that his wagon was there. But they were in great haste, probably escaping from the American army in order to hide in Mexico, where the soldiers could not follow. So my father just lay still in the dark under the wagon, and soon he heard them ride away.

He waited until it was almost dawn. Then he went to see what had happened. He found all of his horses gone, but the Apaches had left their own tired ones behind. So he harnessed the

Apache horses to his freight wagon and went thankfully on his way to Tombstone.

"Did you like that?" asked Lavina. The doll smiled. "So did Miss Hazlem. Someday I hope you can meet Father. Maybe, if I can go home for the summer . . ." She sighed. Summer seemed hopelessly far away.

"Esmeralda is a lovely name," she told the doll. "And it would go with your emerald eyes. But it's taken. I can't name you after a Gila monster."

A few weeks later, Aggie and Lavina came home from school to find a change at 19 Vine Street. The rusty old icebox was gone from Bridget's kitchen, and in its place stood a polished wooden "refrigerator." The refrigerator wasn't actually very different from the icebox; it still required large blocks of ice, which were delivered every week by a big gruff iceman armed with immense tongs. However, the refrigerator was taller, with several individual compartments, and it supposedly kept food colder.

"And, girls," said Bridget, "for supper we're trying something new, entirely."

"What is it?" asked Aggie.

"A surprise," said Bridget.

A clear red substance sparkled in their dessert bowls. Lavina took a spoon and poked: it quivered. It was not a liquid but not quite a solid, either.

Aggie wrinkled her nose.

"Taste it, silly," said her mother. "It's new and delicious."

I Am Lavina Cumming

They each took a spoonful.

"It's called Jell-O," beamed Cousin Maude. "It's ever so much easier than making gelatin the old way."

"I used to boil a calf's foot for hours," said Aunt Agnes.

"Ugh, so messy. This all comes in one little box. There are six flavors, too: strawberry, raspberry, cherry, lemon, orange, and chocolate. That's progress for you."

"What one is this?" asked Lavina.

"'*Which* flavor' would be more correct, Lavina," said Cousin Maude.

"Raspberry, it says on the box," called Bridget from the kitchen. "Sure, it's a lovely red!"

Suddenly Lavina felt starved. She laid down her spoon, and she yearned for the taste of corn, of fresh chiles numbing her tongue, of beef and venison jerky, like edible leather stiff with salt, and of Luz's tortillas, warm, freshly toasted on the Standard Oil can griddle, better than bread.

There were times when Lavina's homesickness became so overpowering that she could almost see it, like fog, or feel the weight of it, like a suitcase. Some days, rainy Sundays especially, Arizona seemed lost and gone forever.

"By the rivers of Babylon, we sat down and wept," intoned the minister from the front of the church, and Lavina gazed sadly down at her folded hands. She had never owned a pair of gloves, white or otherwise, before this winter.

"Wept, when we remembered thee, O Zion . . ."

Tears as sharp as salt crystals stabbed Lavina's eyes. She thought of the Indian captives: How could they ever stop wanting to go home? Father said that they forgot their own families and grew to love their captors. Lavina glanced sideways down the pew. Aunt Agnes stifled a cough in her handkerchief. Cousin Maude readjusted her ear trumpet. Aggie kicked the kneeling rest and received a look of reproof from her grandmother.

"If I forget thee, O Jerusalem, let my right hand forget her cunning. If I do not remember thee, let my tongue cleave to the roof of my mouth . . ."

The rest of the psalm made Lavina feel stronger again, ready to fight like a brave Scot in one of Father's favorite poems; and meanwhile the church service moved grandly on.

"Lift up your hearts."

"We lift them up unto the Lord."

She liked this moment best, before they sank again into the long, long prayers like endless streets, or weeks and months away from home.

In February, after several weeks without a letter, Lavina received an envelope addressed in her oldest brother Tom's handwriting.

> Dear Sis,
>
> We are all fine here except that Father has a bad place on his right hand where a thorn festered, so he can't write. The alfalfa's growing well. After the flood we didn't have to irrigate

for a long time.

Bill and John and I had an adventure. Went hunting with the hounds one night and followed the trail into what we thought was a deserted cabin. Well, it wasn't. The dogs started ki-yi-ing and then we heard men's voices and someone lit a lamp and we saw a sea of dark angry faces who ordered us to get out pronto!

On the floor in the corner we saw a stack of rifles and ammunition. It was a band of Yaqui Indians smuggling arms across the border for that guerrilla war they have going with the Mexicans.

You know how tough the Yaquis are. So we called our hounds out from under the Yaqui dogs and we all high-tailed it out of there! Bill said the Yaquis were as glad to be rid of us as we were to be rid of the Yaquis. Other than that, no news.

Yours, Tom

"Oh, an adventure, and I missed it!" thought Lavina enviously, for she loved to go hunting with her brothers. Their father had taught them all how to shoot a .22 rifle, and sometimes they camped for a few days, which she also loved. They used to tell stories around the campfire and then fall asleep, each snug in a bedroll under the stars.

How unfair that she must live in California and eat Jell-O with a silver spoon while Cousin Maude corrected her grammar! Her brothers' adventure was just like the tale of "Ali Baba and the Forty Thieves," except that the treasure was rifles, not gold, and fortunately nobody was murdered. In Scheherazade's stories, people seemed to lose their heads with great frequency.

"But of course the subject was on her mind," thought Lavina.

It was in the last story of the *Arabian Nights* that Lavina finally discovered a name for her doll.

> The Princess Perizade, who lived with her two older brothers, craved three magical possessions: the Talking Bird, the Golden Water, and the Singing Tree. To find these treasures for her, the brothers climbed a mountain littered with big black stones. But as they climbed they heard threatening voices speaking out of thin air, and when they turned to flee, they too became big black stones.

"Like the Cerro Prieto," thought Lavina.

That was the dark rocky hill behind the ranch. There were no voices on the Cerro, except for the gabble of quail, but there were dangers. Leaning forward, Lavina gripped her pony for dear life with her knees. She dodged the black rocks, the cactus, and the thorny, tangled mesquites that snatched at her hat, clawed her face, ripped her riding skirt. Then it was too steep to ride. She had to get off and leave Chummy if she wanted to reach the top of the hill. She sighed and turned back to her old red book:

So Princess Perizade went alone. But first she cleverly stuffed her ears with cotton, and then, ignoring the terrible voices, she succeeded in climbing the mountain. She never looked behind her till she reached the summit. There she discovered the Talking Bird, who told her how to fill a silver flask with the Golden Water and pluck a twig of the Singing Tree.

"That is not enough," said Princess Perizade. "I must also rescue my brothers."

Finally, reluctantly, the Talking Bird revealed that the Golden Water would break the spell. So the princess walked down the mountain carrying the bird cage, the twig, and the flask, with which she sprinkled every black rock she saw.

Instantly each rock became a man again, all adventurers who had failed to climb the mountain. And at last she found her brothers and released them from the evil spell, and they all lived happily ever after.

From the top of the Cerro Prieto, Lavina could see the Santa Cruz valley, with the river at the bottom shining through the lush green trees and fields, and the different, duller gleam of the tin roof on her father's house. Then at a distance the brown hills began, and the next rows were reddish mountains, then purple, and finally, at a very great distance, pale blue. The top was Lavina's magic place, where Esmeralda the monster visited her. She called the place *La Cima*, the summit. Up there, while Chummy waited patiently, Lavina rested, drank from her canteen, and felt like a queen. Lavinalandia was all around her.

"I will name you Princess Perizade," Lavina told her doll. "But that is your magic name, and we are the only ones who know it."

I Am Lavina Cumming

CHAPTER FOURTEEN
Chinatown

 At last Lavina began to see the first signs of a California spring. The rain stopped; the sun shone mildly. Plants blossomed everywhere, but the fruit trees delighted Lavina most. Their delicate petals burst from bare brown twigs. First came the pink cherry and plum trees, and then, in froths of white, the other plums and the apples and the pears. They looked like enormous bouquets scattered throughout the streets of Santa Cruz.

Cousin Maude arranged some of the flowering branches in tall china jars and placed them around the house.

"There! Isn't that artistic?" she sighed.

Then she went to the piano and sang romantic songs, including "Juanita" (" 'Nita! Juanita! Ask thy soul if we should part . . ."), and "Sweet Adeline," and the girls' favorite: "Come away with me, Lucille, in my merry Oldsmobile . . ." Signor Caruso the canary trilled along with her.

Cousin Maude seemed very cheerful these days.

She had changed the way she did her hair, and she hardly ever used her ear trumpet. However, Aggie was often in a sour mood and spent hours playing with her dolls by herself. Lavina didn't mind, for she much preferred Susan and Birdie as playmates, and when she was feeling homesick, it always cheered her up to visit them.

Susan's father was tall, loose limbed, funny, and hound doggy like Susan, while Mrs. Pitts loved what she called Culture, capitalizing the word with the tone of her voice. She belonged to a ladies' literary club, and the Pitts house was always littered with pictures, newspapers, and books. The Pittses owned a Victrola with a large collection of records, including some of the daring new ragtime songs ("Won't you come home, Bill Bailey, won't you come home?").

But currently Mrs. Pitts was all agog over Grand Opera, and Italian arias poured from the Victrola's flower-shaped horn. The great Italian tenor Enrico Caruso was coming to sing in San Francisco at Easter time, and Mrs. Pitts had set her heart on hearing him.

"It's the chance of a lifetime!" she exclaimed.

Susan was eager to go, too. (Her brother absolutely refused.)

"Of course, Sarah Bernhardt would be even better," Susan told Lavina and Birdie. "I'd *die* to see the divine Sarah."

"But you couldn't see her if you were dead." Birdie's dimples flickered in her circular cheeks.

Birdie and her parents also had tickets. Mrs. Pitts had persuaded Mrs. Lee (who sang in a church choir, and who, besides, was a doting mother to her large brood of children) that all musical people should hear the great Caruso. Mr. Lee, who couldn't carry a tune, was said to have his doubts about Eyetalian singers. But he, too, was an indulgent parent.

Lavina knew that there was no use wanting what she couldn't have. "Oh, well, Susan will act it all out for me afterward," she thought. "That will be almost as good. And funnier."

One Saturday in March, Aunt Agnes came down to breakfast in her walking suit and announced:

"I must go to Watsonville on business today, children. Who would like to come with me?"

"Oh, dear," said Cousin Maude. "I can't. I have to give Freddy his lesson."

Aggie shook her head vigorously. "No. Business is boring, and so is the ride."

"Aggie, tell Grandmama 'No, thank you' nicely," said her mother.

"No-thank-you-Grandmama."

"How about you, Lavina?" asked Aunt Agnes.

"Yes, please," said Lavina. "May I bring my doll?"

"Certainly," said her aunt. "And don't forget a clean handkerchief."

"Yes, ma'am."

They took a cab to Watsonville, where they were met by a Chinese man with a buggy.

"This is Mr. Ah-Toy," said Aunt Agnes. "My niece, Lavina."

Mr. Ah-Toy bowed low, and Lavina, in great confusion, bowed back.

"Mr. Ah-Toy will drive. He is my interpreter," Aunt Agnes explained.

What could this business be? Lavina longed to ask questions, even though she knew that children should be seen and not heard.

"Watsonville!" she thought, looking around. "Here I stood, all by myself."

For an instant it seemed like yesterday. Lavina shuddered and hugged Princess Perizade tightly. The buggy passed through the little town, and soon they were surrounded by blooming orchards. Lavina thought it looked like Fairyland, too pretty to be true. Then they rounded a bend in the road and stopped in front of a cluster of small buildings.

"Where are we?" wondered Lavina. Smoke rose from the chimneys, but she saw no people at all.

Mr. Ah-Toy hitched his horse to a tree and knocked upon the nearest door, which was opened by a Chinese woman with a baby in her arms. They spoke, he gestured toward the buggy, and immediately dozens of Chinese people poured from the houses—men with long pigtails that hung down below their hats, women in sandals and soft trousers, and many children—all chattering at once and pointing. Lavina was certain that they were pointing at her.

"What is this?" she asked, half frightened.

"This is Chinatown," said her aunt calmly.

The storm of voices rose even higher. Mr. Ah-Toy waved his arms and talked back.

"I own it," added Aunt Agnes. "This is the day I collect the rent."

I Am Lavina Cumming

Mr. Ah-Toy came over to the buggy. "They are worried because there are two of you. They tell me to say that they will only pay you, Mrs. Scott, and not Missy. They will only pay once."

"Yes, of course," said Aunt Agnes.

Lavina followed her aunt slowly from door to door as the tenants placed the rent money in her hands. The insides of the cabins were dark, and she noticed strange smells of cooking and of incense. Sticks of incense, set beside two or three shriveled oranges, smoldered in front of little household altars. The children stared at her, and she stared back.

While they were driving back to Watsonville, Lavina noticed several Chinese children at work in the fields and orchards. Aunt Agnes deposited her bag of money in the bank, and then Mr. Ah-Toy helped them into a cab again and bowed low as they drove away. Meanwhile Lavina was thoughtful.

Aunt Agnes sank into her seat with a grateful sigh.

"I have to make this trip every month," she explained. "They won't pay anybody but me."

"So that is how you get your money, Aunt Agnes?"

Her aunt looked at her searchingly through her spectacles. "Some of it. I also own orchards and strawberry fields. I inherited the property when my husband died, many years ago."

"I don't have any money."

"Children don't need money, my dear."

Lavina did not like to contradict Aunt Agnes, so she said nothing, but carefully wrapped one of the

Princess's curls around her own finger. Dolls cost money, just like clothes and railroad tickets, she knew. She thought of the children at work in the fields.

"Parents take care of the money," said Aunt Agnes.

"Father doesn't have much," said Lavina.

Now it was Aunt Agnes's turn to be silent.

"And there was a flood at the ranch, and he has hurt his hand. I wish he would write to me."

"I'll send him a letter tomorrow," said Aunt Agnes. "Douglas was always my favorite brother."

"So when you were children, you never quarreled?" asked Lavina.

Her aunt laughed. "No, child, I cannot say that! All brothers and sisters have their disagreements."

A sad expression crossed her face. "Sometimes this world is a bad place. We must hope for a better world to come, I suppose. But nothing is more important than our families. Blood is thicker than water. We are all Cummings, aren't we?"

She touched Lavina's cheek with her gloved hand.

"I would like to see Douglas again. You know that he used to live here?"

Lavina nodded. "Why did he leave?"

Aunt Agnes looked away, and again her face became troubled. "It was after his first wife died. You did know that he was married before?"

Lavina was stunned. "No! I didn't!"

"Ah!"

Lavina did not dare to ask most of the questions

that filled her mind. Why had Father never told them? What other secrets did he have? What stories had he never told?

"After she died, he went away. To the Indian wars—the gold fields—to Tombstone, of all the dreadful places for a decent Christian to live! But then he settled down again, and you know the rest of it, child."

Suddenly Lavina remembered the smell of the saloon in Tucson.

"I suppose he didn't like to tell you about the sad memories. Why, here we are in Santa Cruz again! Good gracious sakes, what a short journey that was!"

Something extremely surprising was parked in front of 19 Vine Street.

"What on earth—" exclaimed Aunt Agnes, stepping down from the cab.

"It's an automobile," said Lavina. "But whose?"

"No one whom I know has an automobile," said Aunt Agnes majestically.

Cousin Maude whisked open the front door. "It belongs to Mr. Moberley, Mother!"

Behind her they caught a glimpse of Mr. Moberley's mustache.

"Call me Frank," he said.

"It's Frank's," said Cousin Maude, laughing.

Freddy squeezed past her and ran towards the street.

"It's an Oldsmobile," he said. "Isn't it just dandy?"

They gathered around it, even Aggie and Aunt

Agnes, to admire its gleaming black paint and mechanical marvels.

"Curved dashboard, you see," Mr. Moberley pointed out. "And this is how you steer her."

Mr. Moberley rotated the steering wheel, and they all watched the front tires twist from side to side.

"Who wants a ride?" he asked.

"Not today, thank you," said Aunt Agnes. "I believe I am too old for this."

"Me! Me!" shouted Freddy.

"I would," said Lavina.

"I guess so," said Aggie.

"Let's all go," said Mr. Moberley.

"Can I drive, Dad?"

"No, son. In the back you go."

The auto was really only a two seater—a run-about, Mr. Moberley called it—so he and Cousin Maude sat in front and the children squeezed behind the seat. With a pop and a lurch, they set off down the hill. Lavina noticed that the automobile glided more smoothly and evenly than a wagon or carriage, once it built up speed. Stops and starts were still quite jerky.

But there was no connection with another living being, as there always was with a horse. On Chummy's friendly sweaty back, she felt that her own legs were long and strong and that her four feet were hard. Lavina stared at Vine Street without seeing it, lost in a dream.

In the dream she rose before dawn and slipped down to the corral. Chummy came to meet her and took the bit like a carrot. She stood on a rock, grabbed a handful of his mane, and rode off bare-back toward the Bosque. A tall bulky figure stood at the end of the trail.

"Father!" she called, kicking Chummy into a lope.

Mr. Moberley began to sing: "Come away with me, Lucille . . ." His mustache flapped in the breeze.

"You have a nice bass voice, Frank," Cousin Maude told him as they spun along the street, faster and faster. In spite of the noise of the Oldsmobile, she seemed to hear him perfectly. "Really, I need one of those new automobile veils to keep my hair in place."

"Get one, and I'll take you for a long ride, Maude," he said.

"Ow!"

"I didn't touch her."

"He did *so*."

"Mind your manners, children," said Cousin Maude, but she never looked back.

CHAPTER FIFTEEN
Magic,
Black and White

 On Easter Monday, Aunt Agnes allowed Lavina to invite Birdie and Susan over to play. It was a beautiful April morning, a school holiday. Lavina leaned over the front gate of 19 Vine Street as she waited for her friends. Birds sang loudly from the trees. Down in Monterey Bay the ocean glistened, marked here and there with whitecaps, and the waves galloped endlessly onto the beach.

"Everything would be perfect," thought Lavina, "if only I had some news from home."

Then she saw a tall thin shape and a short round one appear at the top of the hill, and she forgot her troubles.

"Yoo-hoo!" Lavina shouted.

Birdie and Susan yoo-hooed back and ran downhill.

When they grew tired of playing outdoors, they went upstairs and sat on Lavina's bed.

"We should have brought our dolls," said Birdie,

glancing at Princess Perizade, who lay in her usual place on Lavina's pillow.

"Oh, we don't need dolls," said Susan. "Let's put on a play!"

Just then Aunt Agnes called, "Lavina!"

She and Cousin Maude stood at the front door, dressed for going out.

"Maudie and I are attending the Women's Christian Temperance luncheon," said Aunt Agnes. "Bridget will be here, if you need anything. And, girls, please include Aggie in your games."

They looked at each other, not daring to object.

"Ta-ta!" said Cousin Maude, and the door closed behind them.

"Awful Aggie," said Susan, under her breath.

"Look," said Birdie. "Here comes the postman."

Lavina ran to get the mail. And there it was at last, a letter from home!

"Read it, Lavina," said Susan.

"Let's go hide in my room."

"Dear Sis," wrote Tom. "I have good news for you. Father is much better." Lavina raced through the letter, her heart pounding. "Worried—thorn in his finger—blood poisoning—doctor in Nogales—no good—whole hand swelled—burning up with fever—afraid—gangrene."

She turned the page. "And then," wrote Tom, "Jim and Bill went for Luz."

> Luz mashed the leaves of a century plant. She laid them on Father's hand, and then she

washed it with some strange tea that she cooked up from a greasewood bush. Father was too sick to say no. The next morning the swelling went down and he started to get well. We think she saved his life.

Father had scrawled a few words after Tom's signature: "Love to Daughtie."

"Oh!" Lavina gasped. How could Father be ill—Father, who was always as strong as the mountains behind the house? She tried to picture his face, and to her dismay she could not quite see him in her mind. The old, safe Father was gone.

"What is it?" asked her friends.

When Lavina explained, Susan said, "But who is Luz?"

"Well," said Lavina, "do you remember that I told you I knew a witch?"

"Luz is a witch?" demanded Susan, her eyes sparkling.

"A good witch," said Lavina stoutly. "A *curandera*, a healer. Well, and she does tell fortunes."

"How?" Birdie's mouth made an O.

"She lives in a little mud house all by herself," said Lavina. "It's dark inside, except for the light from a hole in the roof. And it's full of bundles of herbs and pictures of saints and crystals and paper flowers and feathers and three big glass jars full of water. She looks into them, and she sees the future. Sometimes she can see the past, too. Once, when my mother lost her silver thimble, Luz looked in the water and learned where it was. And she knows the best fairy tales!"

"Tell us one." Birdie plumped herself down cross-legged, leaned her chin on her hands, and waited for Lavina to begin.

Ho'ok Muerta

Once, down along the border, there was a horrible monster, the wickedest of witches, part animal, part human, and part demon. She had claws instead of hands, a pig's face, and a female body. She lived like a wildcat in a cave in the mountains, near a place called Pozo Verde, or Green Well, and she caught deer, antelope, and mountain lions, and ate them and then, because Ho'ok was partly human, she tanned their hides as a woman does.

But she got a taste for human flesh.

Whenever a baby was crying in the little village of Pozo Verde, Ho'ok would come and offer to take it outside to comfort it.

"Let me hold the baby, my grandchildren," she would croon sweetly.

If the parents agreed, she took it away and tore it apart with her claws and ground it on her grinding stone and ate it up!

"Ugh!" Birdie shuddered.

"This can't be true," said Susan.

"Luz said it was," replied Lavina. "But I think it's like Hansel and Gretel. You'll see."

I Am Lavina Cumming

So the people decided to stop her. They went to a great magician called I'itoi, who lived in a cave in a magic mountain called Baboquivari. And I'itoi said, "I will kill Ho'ok."

First, he invited her to a party. There was a feast, and later there was dancing. For three nights in a row he asked her to come and dance with the other people, and she refused. But on the fourth night Ho'ok dressed herself in her finest buckskin and a necklace of dried white bones and came to the great circle of rocks where the people were holding hands and dancing in a ring. She took I'itoi's hand, and she danced, too, with her bone necklace making a weird rattling noise, until she was dizzy. Then he offered her a drugged cigarette, which made her fall into a sound sleep. Nothing could awaken her. And then I'itoi carried the witch to her cave, and the people walled her in and lighted a huge bonfire. When her toes began to burn, Ho'ok awoke.

"No! No! Why have you done this, my grandchildren?" she screamed.

She howled and jumped up and down, cracking open the rocks overhead, but she could not escape. So the children were safe ever afterwards.

And if you go to Pozo Verde, you can still see the circle of rocks where the people danced with Ho'ok, and the cave with a grinding stone in front of it and a crack through the roof, where she was burned to death.

People call that cave Ho'ok Muerta, Dead
Witch.
And it is still smoky.

"The last part is true," said Lavina. "Luz saw the
cave herself."

She could almost hear Luz's low voice and her
special way of talking, half-swallowing the words,
leaving wide spaces between them, while her quick
brown hands patted out tortilla after tortilla.

"Oh," cried Lavina suddenly, "I miss them all so
much!" She flung herself upon her bed. "I want to go
home," she sobbed.

Birdie and Susan patted her on the back sympathetically.

"Wouldn't you miss us, too?" asked Birdie.

"Yes, but Arizona is so far away! I want to see the
Bosque Ranch again!"

"Listen, Lavina," said Susan. "It's not far away at
all. And it never will be. You never can lose it."

"What do you mean?"

"You have it in your heart."

Why, Susan was right, Lavina thought.

The silver river flowed, the ranch house roof glittered, the brown, purple, and blue mountains stood
firmly in their places. Father and the boys waited for
her there forever. And Mama, too.

"Courage," she told herself as she sat up and
wiped her eyes.

"Would you like to see my magic necklace?" she
asked. "Luz made it for me when I left home."

"Oh, yes!" the girls said.

"It's a secret," Lavina warned them. "I'm not supposed to have it anymore. Aunt Agnes took it away from me, but Bridget saved it. And I keep it hidden here."

She unscrewed the knob on the tip of the bedpost, and pulled out the string of colored charms.

"Great Caesar's green galloping ghost!" said Susan.

"Ooh!" sighed Birdie.

"What are these red things?" asked Susan.

"Coral beans."

"Are they good to eat?"

"Dead-ly poi-son," said Lavina in a deep voice.

"Black magic?" asked Susan.

"Not exactly—" Lavina began, but Birdie jumped up.

"Someone's listening!" she whispered, and pointed at the door.

Lavina threw it open. There was Aggie, crouched in the hall.

CHAPTER SIXTEEN
Queen

 "What are you doing?" cried Birdie.

Lavina felt a chill at her heart, and almost unconsciously she stuffed the necklace into her pocket. On the wall behind Aggie, the picture of Love, squeezing her cherubs, gazed down from her frame.

"Nothing," said Aggie sullenly. "I just wanted to *play*."

The older girls looked at one another. How much had she overheard? Had she actually seen the necklace? Would she tattle?

"Did you hear what I was saying?" demanded Lavina.

A pause. "No."

Was she telling the truth? Lavina couldn't tell from the expression in Aggie's eyes, as hard and shiny and blank as two blue glass marbles.

"We'd better let her play," Lavina said at last.

"Aggie," said Susan in a thrilling voice, "it's a

terrible thing to tell other people's secrets. Girls who do that . . . pay a dreadful price."

Aggie's marble eyes shifted from Susan to Birdie to Lavina, but she admitted nothing.

"I want to play dress-up," she said.

"Maybe she doesn't know anything," thought Lavina.

"Dress up in what?" said Birdie.

Aggie pointed at the door of the room next to Lavina's—the real attic, which Aunt Agnes called the storeroom. Lavina had never done more than peep at the stacks of old furniture and wooden boxes inside.

"There's a trunk full of old clothes in there. My grandmama lets me dress up in them whenever I want."

Susan's eyes shone, for she loved costumes. "Let's take a look."

Aggie led the way. A tarnished brass key stood in the lock of an old-fashioned leather trunk. Aggie turned the key, raised the creaky lid of the trunk, and pulled out a crumpled black taffeta bonnet. Beneath it lay a fur muff and a pair of yellow, shriveled kid gloves.

"What's this?" asked Lavina. "A hoop skirt?"

It was a contraption of wires, like a bird cage, around a sort of cushion, attached to the back of what seemed to be a belt.

"I know," said Birdie. "My great-aunt Melissa has one in *her* attic. It's a bustle. Ladies used to wear them, to hold out the back of their gowns."

Susan buckled on the bustle and pranced around the storeroom, making the others laugh.

Then Lavina discovered an ivory fan with broken sticks, and Susan discarded the bustle in favor of a lace scarf.

"I'm a Spanish lady," she said, and struck a pose.

"Like the opera," said Birdie. "Oh, I can hardly wait!"

That very night was the great one. Birdie's and Susan's parents were taking their daughters to hear Caruso sing in the opera *Carmen*.

"Papa and Mama say that the Grand Opera House is magnificent," sighed Birdie.

They also planned to spend the night in a hotel.

"My mama is going, too," said Aggie, and a shadow crossed her face.

Mr. Moberley had invited Cousin Maude to go (in the Oldsmobile) to hear Caruso in a matinee performance of another opera, *La Bohème*.

"But *I* don't care about it. *I* hate singing. I hate—" Aggie broke off.

Lavina was silent.

"I'd rather be on the stage than in the audience," said Susan. She floated forward, her nose in the air. "Ladies and gentlemen, I give you the extraordinary, the incomparable—Miss—Susan—Pitts. Ugh! That name!"

"My mother says every little girl wants to change her name," observed Birdie in her placid way.

"Maybe you don't have to change it much," said Lavina. "Susannah Pitts—how about that?"

"Still awful."

"Let's practice speaking our pieces for the end-of-school program," suggested Birdie, practical as usual.

"But I don't have one," said Aggie.

"You can be the audience," said Susan, and she launched into the long and tragic verses of "The Boy Stood on the Burning Deck."

"That was good," said Lavina, when Susan's arms finally stopped waving and dropped to her sides. "But I like you best when you're funny."

"You're next, Lavina," Birdie said.

Lavina's piece was short.

"My heart leaps up," she began, "when I behold a rainbow in the sky . . ."

The little poem reminded her of summer afternoons at home. First a violent thunderstorm washed the desert country clean, and then the sun began to sink behind the Atascosa Mountains, west of the Bosque Ranch. Then, suddenly, a rainbow would spring from north to south across the cloudy sky, its pure colors unlike any others, anywhere.

> So was it when my life began;
> So is it now I am a man;
> So be it when I shall grow old,
>   Or let me die!

"I'm tired of this," Aggie interrupted. "I want to play dress-up. I have naturally curly golden hair, and I want to be *queen*."

"All right," Birdie said. "This paisley shawl can be your cape, and here's a necklace."

"I need a crown," said Aggie.

"Try this old pudding pan," said Susan, and she balanced it on Aggie's curls. The pan actually did resemble a crown, but Aggie shook it angrily onto the floor.

"I want a *good* crown!"

Again, the older girls looked at one another.

"I could make you one," said Birdie, who was used to amusing her many little brothers and sisters.

"How?"

"Well, I need colored paper and scissors and glue."

"All right," said Aggie, appeased. "I have paper and scissors in my room."

"And Bridget can get us the glue pot," said Lavina.

Birdie quickly fashioned a tall silver crown studded with paper rubies and emeralds. Delighted, Aggie put it on and preened. But the crown was too large, and it tumbled over one of Aggie's eyes. She looked ridiculous. A giggle escaped from Lavina, and Aggie's face grew stormy.

"Fix it!"

"I'll try," said Birdie.

She fiddled with the crown, but it was still too large. Aggie stamped her foot.

"You're doing this on purpose," she said. "You'd *better* fix it, or else . . ."

"Or else what?" asked Lavina. Her patience was draining away. How she would love to take Aggie by her skinny shoulders and shake her until her teeth rattled and her famous curls tangled!

"I don't know what," Aggie teased.

Birdie snipped the crown apart and reglued it.

"Just wait a moment, now, till it's dry," she said.

"I want to be queen *now*!" said Aggie.

Lavina heard the sound of the ocean roar through her ears, and immediately she felt warm and enormously powerful.

"I'll fix it," she snapped. She seized the glue pot and dabbed the brush full of the pungent yellow substance. As Birdie and Susan watched in fascination, shocked yet amused, Lavina painted a sticky ring of glue all around the inner surface of the crown.

"Try *that*," she said, and set the crown on Aggie's head.

Aggie was so busy admiring herself in the mirror that she didn't notice anything odd about the crown. Right away she set about playing queen.

"Bow!" she ordered. "You must obey my royal commands."

They tried not to snicker as she sat in an old red velvet armchair and said, "The queen wants candy."

Susan played along: "Your Majesty, we must ask the royal hired girl."

"Very well," said Aggie. "Do it."

They all trooped downstairs, and Bridget provided cookies, along with a keen and quizzical look.

"I'm the queen," boasted Aggie.

"Are you now," said Bridget. "And queen of what, may I ask? The Cannibal Islands, is it?"

"No, no, no," shrieked Aggie wildly. "Queen of *them*. They must do my bidding!"

The older girls tired of this game long before Aggie did. Fear of what she might do, however, kept them from rebellion. Finally they heard the front door open, and the thump-step of a crutch.

"Mama! Mama!" cried Aggie, racing to meet them. "Look at me!"

"Why, you're a lovely queen," said Cousin Maude, somewhat absently.

Aunt Agnes asked where the crown came from.

"They made it for me," said Aggie. "See the jewels?"

"I see that you have been in my old trunk," said her grandmother. "Next time, it would be better to ask permission first."

"Mrs. Scott," said Susan, "excuse me please, I'm sorry about opening the trunk without asking, and thank you for a nice time, but Birdie and I have to go home now because we're supposed to go to the City to see Caruso, and my mother will raise the roof if we're late, and thank you again, good-bye."

"I don't care," called Aggie after them. "I'm sick of this ugly old crown anyway."

"Now, is that nice?" said Cousin Maude, but not as if she really expected Aggie to answer.

Meanwhile, Lavina watched Aggie reach up and try to remove the silver crown. And in fact she lifted it slightly from her head, but no farther. The top layer of her curls lifted with it. Aggie let out a scream—the same sort of infuriated shriek that she uttered when her mother combed her hair into ringlets.

"What's the matter?" asked Cousin Maude.

Aggie's face was almost purple. "They did it to me!" She pointed a shaky finger at Lavina. "*She* did it!"

"Did what?" said Aunt Agnes, with some impatience.

"They *glued* my crown to my *head!*" wailed Aggie. "Now I'll *never* get it off!"

CHAPTER SEVENTEEN
The Pearl-handled Derringer

 At first they pulled gently on the crown. Then they held Aggie's head over the kitchen sink and applied warm water and soap. And then they tugged harder, but nothing helped. Aggie began to sob. Lavina stood by as though hypnotized, and for a while nobody paid any attention to her, or to Aggie's accusations.

"Kerosene might dissolve it," suggested Bridget helpfully. "It kills lice entirely."

At this, Aggie sobbed louder and kicked Bridget in the shins.

"Aggie!" said her mother.

"She will apologize, Bridget," said Aunt Agnes, beginning to look as ruthless as a hawk. Lavina backed away quietly into a corner and waited for the sky to fall on her.

"Lavina did it because she hates me. I saw her put the glue on."

"Be quiet, child," said Aunt Agnes. She turned to her daughter. "You may have to cut her hair, Maude."

Aggie's sobs rose to an even higher pitch.

"She did, she did! Why won't anybody ever believe me? She did something else, too, something even worse!"

Aunt Agnes sank down into a kitchen chair and leaned her chin upon her crutch. Slowly she moved her hazel eyes, magnified by her spectacles, from face to face around the kitchen: Bridget indignant, but still trying to conceal a smile; Cousin Maude bewildered; Aggie in a tantrum; and Lavina paralyzed in the corner beside the refrigerator.

"Lavina disobeyed you, Grandmama. She *kept* that dirty old necklace that you told her to throw away. She hides it in her bed. *She's* the bad girl, not me!"

Aunt Agnes's eyebrows shot up, but when she spoke her voice was calm.

"Lavina," she said, "I have always found you to be truthful. What happened?"

"I did put extra glue on the crown," Lavina confessed. "She fussed so much because it was too big that she made me mad. But I thought the glue would wash out. I never thought the crown would stick so tight. I'm sorry."

Aunt Agnes blinked once or twice, and Lavina even thought she saw her aunt's firm mouth give a twitch of amusement. Then her expression grew fierce once again.

"Now what about the rest of this? Do you have that necklace in your bed, Lavina?"

Lavina gulped. Across the room she saw Bridget's dismay, and she realized that she was not the only

I Am Lavina Cumming

one in trouble. But could she lie to Aunt Agnes?

"No, ma'am," she said.

"Yes, she does!" squawked Aggie.

"I have it here," Lavina said, and she held out her hand to her aunt.

Aunt Agnes looked from the necklace to Bridget. "But did I not ask you to dispose of this, Bridget?"

"You did, ma'am," Bridget answered. A rosy flush spread over her cheekbones.

"And you disobeyed my orders?"

"I hadn't the heart to do it, ma'am. There she was, poor mite, all alone in the world, nary a scrap to remind her of home. And was I to be tossing an image of the Blessed Virgin in the ash can, ma'am? No, I couldn't do it, not me!" At the end of this speech Bridget threw her apron over her head and burst into tears herself.

"You must leave my service," said Aunt Agnes, at her most hawkish. Her nostrils flared. "Lavina, hand over the necklace. Then go upstairs to the storeroom, which I am sure is untidy, and put it straight. Afterward you may go to your room until I decide what to do with you."

As though in a dream, Lavina laid the little heap of coral beans, feathers, and blue glass beads upon the kitchen table. The medallion glittered faintly, and so did Aunt Agnes's spectacles. Nobody said a word, not even Aggie. Then Lavina walked slowly out the door and up the stairs. As in certain kinds of nightmares, there seemed to be no possibility of hurry.

She lay on her bed for the rest of the afternoon, holding Princess Perizade and listening for noises from below. Only once before had she ever been in so much trouble, and that was last year, soon after Mama died.

Father owned several guns, which the children were forbidden to touch, unless, of course, they were learning to shoot them under Father's guidance. In the Bosque ranch house, he kept a six-shooter and a couple of rifles and an ancient shotgun. But there was another gun that he never used, which he kept in a locked drawer, and which was especially forbidden to Lavina and her brothers.

It was a little pearl-handled derringer, a tiny short-barreled pocket pistol that Father had acquired somewhere in his earlier, wilder life—perhaps in Virginia City, Nevada, where once he'd passed some time, or perhaps in Tombstone. The pearl-handled derringer was rather a mystery around the Cumming house. It did not seem to fit the Father that the children knew. Since it was pretty and attractive, like a toy, Father was unusually careful of it; and therefore when Lavina and John discovered one day that the drawer was unlocked, they could not resist the temptation to take it out and play with it.

Father found them.

A pale gray shadow fell over the grass where she and John sat playing with the little pistol. Father's thick hand reached down and seized the gun; she saw the way his skin was cracked around the knuckles from hard work. She saw his nostrils flare. But before he even scolded or paddled them, he leaned back and threw the pearl-handled derringer as hard and as far as he could, way out into the center of the

I Am Lavina Cumming

Santa Cruz River, where it sank with a small plop. And Lavina knew that she would remember that lesson until the end of her life.

But in that scrape, at least she was not alone. John was just as guilty as she was, and soon he was cracking jokes, and after that, except for their sore bottoms, they were comfortable again.

"If only Aunt Agnes had just spanked me!" said Lavina to Princess Perizade, who smiled the same way as usual. "But I guess that's not the ladylike way to punish people."

She would never be a lady. Clearly, it took more than new clothes and a few months of practice. Lavina waited and waited. She sang Spanish lullabies to Princess Perizade. She stared at the picture of Mount Vesuvius until she had memorized every detail. At long last, there was a tap on her door, and Bridget appeared with a supper tray.

"Oh, Bridget, I'm so sorry," Lavina lamented.

"Never you mind, dearie," Bridget said. "You did your best, and so did I. I don't regret it. Mark my words, though, I think your auntie will, when she cools down. She's gone to rest while Mrs. Temple works on that brat Aggie's hair."

"What happened?"

Bridget sat down on the bed and folded her hands. "I'm to leave in the morning. At first she said I had to go right then, but then she reconsidered, said she wanted to be fair, wouldn't tell my next employer, and so on. But I don't care. Maybe it's a good thing, really. Maybe I won't have another mistress. There's a certain gentleman, you see, who's been askin' me to marry him, and maybe now I'll say yes."

"Oh, Bridget! But what about me?"

Bridget looked concerned and reached out a rough hand to smooth the hair back from Lavina's forehead.

"You're to stay in your room this evening, that's all I know. Mrs. Temple, now, she said to send you home."

"I'd like that," said Lavina. But then suddenly she wondered if she really would. What would Father say? And there were things about California and Aunt Agnes's house that she would miss, she realized. She would be very sorry not to finish the year with Miss Hazlem's class.

"I don't know what will happen," said Bridget, and she gave Lavina a big hug. "I'm sorry to say good-bye. But never say die, dearie. There's a good time coming, you'll see."

Lavina lay under her quilt and waited for sleep to arrive. Princess Perizade's brown curls tickled her cheek, and she thought of Aunt Agnes's kindness in giving the doll to her, and her terrible wrath now. These problems were too serious for tears; they required careful thought instead.

She remembered the story of Juan and Juanita. As the Comanches slept, the children tiptoed away . . .

"Maybe I will run away," Lavina thought. "I can't afford a train ticket, but I can work. Cook, scrub, iron—I used to do all the things Bridget does. Or if I could get to Watsonville, maybe I could work in the strawberry fields or the apple orchards. The Chinese

I Am Lavina Cumming

children do. And then I would move south, toward Arizona . . . I'm strong, like a little mustang, Father always says. Father. What would he think? Would he be angry at me?"

She rolled over and tried to see Father in her memory. At last a picture took shape in her mind, but the figures were small and their hats shaded their faces. It was like the photograph that Father had sent for Christmas.

"After all," she thought suddenly, "*he* was the one who sent me here."

She lay with her eyes open in the dark, conscious of herself, Lavina Cumming, warm and solid in the bed, and alone.

"I can walk a long way. How could I hunt? Juan and Juanita had a dog, and a bow and arrows. Still, in California there's so much fruit to eat . . . I'll get up early and pack my bag and leave before anyone wakes up," she decided at last.

And then, her plans laid, she fell asleep.

CHAPTER EIGHTEEN
5:13 A.M.,
April 18, 1906

Out of the quiet, Lavina heard screams. It was a massacre. Blood on the rocks. A strange man threw her across the neck of his horse, and she clutched desperately at the harsh mane. Then the horse turned into Chummy, and she was alone, and he was trying to buck her off. He whinnied shrilly and reared.

She awoke in the dark, rigid with fear. The horse's scream was still in her ears.

"A nightmare!" she thought.

But her bed was really moving. It rolled on its casters from one side of her bedroom to the other, all by itself. The house was moving! She heard it creak and moan. She bounced off the opposite side of her room; she heard her washstand mirror shatter under the impact of the iron bed. A rain of plaster showered down from the walls.

Lavina grabbed Princess Perizade and held her tightly as their bed continued to roll like a crazy automobile. She heard crashes both inside Aunt

Agnes's house and outside in the yard and the street. Glass splintered and heavy objects thudded to the ground. The sky seemed to be falling. The whole world moved, the ground heaved like the ocean, and Lavina began to feel sick at her stomach.

Downstairs some person shrieked.

Lavina and the doll rode back and forth across the bedroom twice again, and then came a louder crash than any of the others, upon the roof directly above Lavina's head. Her window shattered; something hit the floor inside her room. She burrowed into her covers, hiding her eyes and ears from the fearsome chaos.

"Is this the end of the world?" Lavina thought. "Judgment Day? Am I dying? Or maybe already dead? Is it—can it be—because of what I did to Aggie? Or because of the necklace?"

Abruptly it was over. There was a moment of silence, and the scream came again, followed by more distant screams and shouts next door and throughout the neighborhood.

"Why, it was an earthquake," Lavina said to herself. Now she remembered that people had mentioned California earthquakes to her before. But she had imagined a quake would be like a nearby clap of thunder, giving everybody a start and rattling the dishes a little, perhaps. Not like this.

"Mama, Mama!" The voice was Aggie's. *She* had survived.

"Well," thought Lavina, "Bad or not, I'm here, too. I think I'll get up."

Her bed was full of powdery bits of smashed

plaster. Cautiously she sat up and brushed herself off, tucked her doll under her arm, and touched a toe on the floor.

"Broken glass," she said aloud.

She considered for a moment. This was like dealing with rattlesnakes, she thought. You must be careful, not scared, and use your head. What time was it? Very early morning, she guessed. A weak light was seeping into the sky. She managed to hook one of her shoes with her bare toe, and then she hopped over to the other one, braced all the while for more sickening, surging earthquakes, but none came. Now she saw what had broken her window; a brick lay in the middle of her room. The kitchen chimney had collapsed onto the roof above her, and that was why a big crack ran across her ceiling. The air that streamed through the broken window was cold and clammy.

"My coat," said Lavina.

She heard people moving around downstairs. Bridget's voice called, "Mrs. Scott! Mrs. Temple! Are you all right? Lavina?"

Lavina opened her door, which sagged oddly from its hinges, and picked her way gingerly from stair step to stair step. By the dawn light she saw that Faith, Hope, Charity, and Love had fallen from their places. On the second floor landing, the marble lady lay flat on her face, and her vase of flowers was smashed. The water from the vase soaked slowly into the carpet, making a dark red stain. Behind her bedroom door Aggie continued to scream, but just as Lavina crept toward it, Cousin Maude emerged dizzily from her own room.

Bridget's red head popped up above the lower banister. "Is Aggie hurt? Go to her, Mrs. Temple, and I'll see about your mother."

Aunt Agnes! Where was she? For the first time since the earthquake—since last night—Lavina found herself able to move fast. She beat Bridget to the door. Her aunt's bedroom, crowded with antique furniture and precious knickknacks, had become a shambles. The four-poster bed lay upside down; the old lady must be pinned underneath.

"Aunt Agnes!" Lavina tugged frantically at the bed frame and succeeded in moving it aside just as Bridget came to help. Together they pulled away the mattress and discovered Aunt Agnes, as pale as her own sheets, lying at the bottom. But she was still breathing, and when they lifted her up, her hazel hawk eyes, looking tender and unfamiliar without their spectacles, opened.

"Oh, my dears," she said. She put an arm around each of their necks, and they all struggled to their feet together.

"Oof!" puffed Aunt Agnes, sounding more like herself. "This is a fine mess!"

"Let's go. Quick, before the house falls on our heads," warned Bridget.

"Yes . . ." Aunt Agnes looked vaguely around the wreck of her bedroom. "I don't suppose anyone sees my spectacles?"

"Can't wait for that, ma'am."

"My crutch?" said Aunt Agnes.

"No, ma'am, not now. We'll help you. Come on, Lavina, do."

I Am Lavina Cumming

Lavina snatched a blanket from the bed and wrapped it around her aunt. All this time, Aggie's wild screaming had continued, and now Aunt Agnes paused to ask about her granddaughter.

"She looks all right," called Cousin Maude in a high, trembling voice. "But I can't get her to listen to me or come with me."

"Hysteria," snapped Aunt Agnes. "Make her, Maude."

"No, Mama, no, no, no, Mama!"

"We'll come back for her, Mrs. Scott," pleaded Bridget.

"Drag her," said Aunt Agnes.

"Ma'am, I can't."

"Maude certainly can't," said Aunt Agnes in exasperation. Stooped over without her crutch, Aunt Agnes looked Lavina straight in the eye. Or perhaps, Lavina thought in a weird moment of detachment, she herself had grown taller overnight.

"You, Lavina. Go in there and get your cousin. Right now! Come along, Maude. It's dangerous to remain here. Bridget is quite right."

Aunt Agnes grasped the banister and, with Bridget's help, started downstairs at a brisk pace. Then another tremor rocked the house, as though 19 Vine Street were only a leaky rowboat on a stormy sea.

Aggie's room was a small scene of horror: dolls had been tossed everywhere, like miniature dead bodies. Aggie cowered on the floor beside her bed, where Lavina guessed she'd been thrown when the first big quake came. For a second Lavina hardly recognized her cousin; the crown was gone, but her hair was utterly snarled. It stood out in a rat's nest around her head, and she was making strange whooping noises.

"Aggie," Lavina said tentatively, "take my hand."

"No, no, no!"

The house gave another heave. Lavina hauled off and slapped Aggie as hard as she could, which, after years of chopping wood, riding horseback, and playing baseball with her brothers, was fairly hard. Aggie gasped and burst into tears. But they were just ordinary tears, not the crazy shrieks of hysteria, and then Aggie allowed Lavina to lead her safely downstairs and into Aunt Agnes's garden. The second tremor was less violent than the first and subsided more quickly.

They gathered on the cracked sidewalk, all dressed in their nightclothes and beginning to shiver in the chilly air of sunrise. Then they looked down over the tiers of buildings between Vine Street and Monterey Bay and saw yet another terrible and wonderful phenomenon. The bay went dry. Just for an instant, all its water drew back into the ocean and paused, held by a great invisible force. And then it came roaring back in one tremendous wave taller than the hills. As they watched, the tidal wave exploded upon the beach and licked away a row of buildings that had stood at the edge of the sand.

"Let us pray," said Aunt Agnes.

They knelt on the ground and Aunt Agnes's calm voice rose above the clamor all around:

"O Lord our Heavenly Father, who hast safely

brought us to the beginning of this day; defend us in the same with thy mighty power—"

One of the oak trees across the street fell slowly onto the house beside it. After the noise had subsided, Aunt Agnes went on.

"Grant that this day we fall into no sin; neither run into any kind of danger; but that all our doings, being ordered by thy governance, may be righteous in thy sight. Amen."

"Amen," said Bridget clearly.

"Amen," said Cousin Maude.

"Amen," whispered Aggie. Her face was streaked with tears and plaster dust.

"Amen," said Lavina. Hugging Princess Perizade, she watched the sticks and boards that had once been buildings float away into the sea.

"I guess I won't run away today after all," she thought.

CHAPTER NINETEEN
Aftershocks

 Little tremors, or aftershocks, continued to rattle Santa Cruz throughout that whole long day. At first, as the sun rose over the town, Lavina and her family huddled together for warmth, still too stunned to do anything more. They could see their neighbors camped on every lawn nearby. Then Lavina noticed that Bridget's clothes were streaked with blood.

"Are you hurt?" she cried.

"Not much."

Aunt Agnes peered short-sightedly at the cut in Bridget's right hand.

"We must attend to this," she said.

"Oh, I'm freezing," murmured Cousin Maude, who was dressed in a thin, lacy nightgown. The wind must be blowing straight through it, Lavina thought, and she looked down at herself.

"Aunt Agnes," she said, "I'm the only one with shoes. And the house hasn't fallen down yet. What if I went back in and got more blankets?"

Her aunt hesitated. "I don't want to send you into danger, child."

Lavina handed her coat to Cousin Maude. "I'll run fast," she promised.

"Very well, then."

Lavina raced inside and brought out an armload of bedding, and Aunt Agnes tore strips from a pillowcase to bandage Bridget's hand.

"See," Lavina told Aggie, "with this extra sheet we can make ourselves a tent under the plum tree. That's fun."

"I'm hungry." The small listless voice was quite unlike Aggie's usual whine.

As time passed, and the house did not collapse, Lavina made bolder raids inside. She rescued Signor Caruso, who sat in a feathery huff on the bottom of his cage. Then she went to explore the kitchen and returned with a basket of food.

"I smell gas," she reported.

"The pipe may have broken," said Cousin Maude.

"Saints above!" cried Bridget. "We'll all be blown to glory!"

And suddenly they all smelled smoke. Clouds of it curled above the trees on the other side of Santa Cruz, and shouts rang through the neighborhood.

"Fire! Fire!"

Now a few horses and buggies were moving up and down Vine Street, and neighbors in nightclothes came to call.

"We heard the City is ruined," someone said.

"Yes, San Francisco is burning," someone else added.

I Am Lavina Cumming

"Oh!" Lavina clapped her hands to her mouth. "Susan and Birdie!"

"I wonder how the Moberleys are," said Cousin Maude.

Aunt Agnes said steadily, "My dears, we must shut off the gas valve at the street, this minute."

From her chair, where she sat regally wrapped in her blanket, the old lady surveyed her raggle-taggle household.

"We look like a band of gypsies," Aunt Agnes chuckled.

Over her nightgown, Cousin Maude wore one of Bridget's shawls and a kitchen apron. Bridget wore her own best coat, a stylish feathered hat, and bandages. Lavina was wrapped in another of Bridget's shawls, and Aggie, with her frightful hair, wore Lavina's coat.

"Lavina," Aunt Agnes went on, "now that the gas leak seems to have stopped, will you please try to find—" Aunt Agnes ticked the items off on her fingers: "my spectacles and a clean handkerchief. And if you happen across it, my sewing basket. Oh, and a comb."

After spending some time searching, Lavina finally carried the items out to her aunt. One spectacle lens was slightly cracked, but Aunt Agnes wiped them with the handkerchief and placed them on her nose with a sigh of relief. She opened the sewing basket and selected a pair of scissors.

"Now!" she said. "Aggie, come here."

Cousin Maude and Aggie both winced, but Aggie

obeyed her grandmother without saying a word.

Snip! A long lock of the hopeless hair fell to the ground. Click! Another one followed. And in a very short time Aggie was shorn.

"She looks like a chick just sprouting pin feathers," Lavina thought.

Aggie put her hand wonderingly up to her head and touched the short blond tufts that remained.

"Much better," said her grandmother.

"No more ringlets," mourned her mother.

"No more ringlets," repeated Aggie in a faraway tone. And then she smiled. "No more combing!"

"It feels so *light*," she said next. She gave a little skip. She turned to Lavina and smiled again. "Thank you," she said.

Lavina sat down bump on the grass in utter amazement.

Aunt Agnes said, "Lavina, I owe you an apology."

Lavina shook her head until her pigtails batted her shoulders. "It was wrong of me to keep the necklace without telling you. But I didn't know how to explain. I felt homesick, and poor, and bad."

Aunt Agnes removed her spectacles and polished them again.

"We won't say another word about it, child. All's well that ends well. Now, Bridget," said Aunt Agnes crisply. "You have been a true heroine today, you and Lavina both. I am a cross old woman. I hope that you will both forgive what I said last night and stay on with us."

"Yes, please stay," said Cousin Maude.

"Please," said Aggie.

A wonderful warmth glowed in Lavina's heart. She felt as she had felt at the end of her journey to California, when Aunt Agnes first opened her door and welcomed Lavina inside.

"Well, ma'am," began Bridget. A grin broke out all over her face, and she raised her bandaged hand. "I can't exactly cook for you right now."

"I can!" said Lavina, jumping up.

"No, dear, it's not safe," said her aunt.

"We'll build a campfire," said Lavina. "I know all about it. We do it on roundups and when we go hunting. Let's have bacon and eggs, that's easy, and I can even bake biscuits in a Dutch oven, or gingerbread."

"I like gingerbread," said Aggie in her new small voice.

Lavina made a circle of bricks from the fallen chimney and sent Aggie to collect tinder and twigs for a fire.

"Father taught me how to build a one-match fire when I was little," she said.

First she stood the smallest twigs in a pyramid over a few dry leaves and bits of paper, and then she built several gradually larger pyramids over the first one.

"There!"

The match flared; the fire blazed; the bacon sizzled in the pan. Lavina boiled water for tea. Aggie brought firewood. She watched intently as Lavina mixed flour, ginger, butter, molasses, eggs, and hot water, then filled the hot Dutch oven with gingerbread batter, set the iron lid in place, and buried the Dutch oven in the coals.

"When is it done?"

"When it smells done," said Lavina. "Not for a while. We'll eat it for supper." She settled down by the fire with a sigh of contentment. "See, Aggie—when you don't have chairs, you squat. Try it. It works just fine."

"Every fire is different," she thought, staring into the flames, "yet all fires are the same."

She saw an Arizona campfire. Soon the day's work would be done, and her brothers would gather around, and after they had eaten their beans and tortillas and meat, they would all listen quietly in the smoky firelight.

"What kind of story do you want?"

"A true story, Father!"

Suddenly Lavina heard the rude honk of an automobile horn.

"Frank!" cried Cousin Maude, and she dashed to the curb.

　　　　　　　　　　I Am Lavina Cumming

CHAPTER TWENTY
Gingerbread

 The Oldsmobile chugged up the hill, with Freddy waving from the passenger seat. Mr. Moberley was as sooty as a chimney sweep.

"I've been fighting fires," he called as they drew closer. "Twelve buildings completely gone in Santa Cruz, they say. But that's nothing compared to the City."

"Oh, Birdie! Susan!" thought Lavina.

When Mr. Moberley stepped from the car, Cousin Maude threw her arms around him.

"I've been awfully worried, Frank."

"You worried about me, really?" said Mr. Moberley.

"Of course, and Freddy, too. How are you, dear?"

Freddy was staring at Aggie.

"What happened to *her*?" he said.

"Nothing to do with the earthquake," sniffed Aggie. She tossed her head, but nothing in particular happened.

"Well," thought Lavina, "at least he can't pull her hair anymore and shout 'ding-dong!'"

"Can you stay to dinner?" asked Cousin Maude. "We'd be ever so delighted."

Mr. Moberley accepted.

"Is there enough bacon?" whispered Lavina to Bridget.

"There's plenty of eggs," said Bridget. "I'm sure I don't know why they didn't break in the earthquake."

"Look! Look!" shouted Freddy and Aggie, jumping up and down and pointing.

A bedraggled group of refugees had appeared at the bottom of the Vine Street hill. There were two men in nightshirts tucked into their trousers; one woman in a nightgown, a string of pearls, and a man's coat; and another woman elegantly dressed in an evening gown and an opera cloak, with tattered bedroom slippers on her feet. A tall thin girl wore pajamas and a woman's fur stole. A short chubby girl wore what seemed to be two nightgowns and a checked tablecloth. They grinned through the grime on their faces.

Lavina started to run.

"Susan! Birdie! Yoo-hoo!"

The Pittses and the Lees sank down on Aunt Agnes's lawn and all spoke at once.

"In the beginning, we were all thrown out of bed," said Susan's father.

"We were, too," said Freddy.

"My bed took me for a ride," said Lavina.

"And the hotel was in a panic. Luckily ours stood the shock pretty well; some of those skyscrapers collapsed immediately. I tell you, San Francisco will never be the same again."

"The Grand Opera House is gone," said Mrs. Pitts sadly. "And churches, mansions, boardinghouses, everything. Soldiers are dynamiting buildings to try to stop the fire, but it's burning out of control."

"Oh, no!"

Mr. Lee shook his head. "We were very lucky. Among the first to escape from the City."

"But first we had to walk through the ruins," said Susan.

"Oh, it was terrible," said Birdie.

"Such awful sights," said her mother. She covered her face briefly with her hands, as though she were praying.

Many voices spoke at once:

"There was a man walking down Market Street with an empty bird cage in his hand."

"There were mothers who had lost their children, and children without mothers."

"I saw a little dressmaker pushing her sewing machine along through the rubble. It was all she had."

"There were robbers. There were soldiers with bayonets. Firemen. Heroes. People drinking champagne. People thirsty."

"Boom, boom, boom from the dynamite, all the time."

"The water mains are broken, so they can't fight the fires very well. The telegraph lines are down, and the trains aren't running. San Francisco is entirely cut off from the rest of the world. Food is already scarce.

The buildings lean every which way; the streets are so full of wreckage that it's like walking over the roughest mountains."

The chorus of voices fell silent for a moment.

"Oh, my poor feet," said Mrs. Lee.

"How did you ever get out?" asked Mr. Moberley.

"We decided to leave immediately, and by water instead of train," said Mr. Pitts. "We gathered some clothes—as you see!—and made our way to the Ferry Building."

"Oh, Lavina," breathed Susan. "We walked through Chinatown, where all the buildings had fallen down. And underneath the streets were tunnels—so strange."

"Opium dens," said her father shortly.

Lavina imagined strange fumes rising from cracks in the earth, Chinese altars, children with long pigtails.

"Papa bought food at a little restaurant early in the morning," Birdie said.

"All they had to sell was apple pie and ginger beer! So that's what we lived on, all day long!" laughed Mr. Lee.

"We squeezed onto a ferryboat, crossed the Bay to Oakland, and finally took a train the long way round. And here we are."

"We telephoned our houses from the station," said Mrs. Pitts. "By some miracle, the lines are working. And everyone is all right there."

"Thank God," said Aunt Agnes.

Now dusk was falling, and they drew closer to the fire. A few stars pricked through the sky, almost

I Am Lavina Cumming

the first stars Lavina had noticed since she came to California.

"We'll camp out tonight," said Lavina to her friends. "I'll show you how to make a warm bedroll, and maybe we can sleep in the fort under the plum tree."

"Can I come, too?" asked Freddy.

"Why not?" she said. She glanced at Aggie, but Aggie leaned against Cousin Maude and said nothing.

"Tomorrow," said Mr. Lee, "the work begins."

"Everyone has losses." Aunt Agnes looked grave.

"Tomorrow we'll start to clean up the mess," said Susan's mother, with a sigh.

"And we'll telegraph Lavina's father to say she's safe."

"But there's something you haven't told us," said Mr. Moberley.

"What's that?"

"How was the opera?"

"Oh!" The adults broke into laughter. "Fine, just fine. It seems so long ago."

"And the great Caruso?" said Cousin Maude.

"Well," said Mr. Pitts, "the last I saw of him was early this morning. He was in his shirtsleeves, sitting on top of a heap of trunks in a freight wagon. He looked like a lost soul."

"He's awfully fat," Susan whispered to Lavina.

"He sang beautifully, anyhow, and he will again," said Mrs. Pitts warmly.

"But not here. The opera season is over, I think," said Mr. Moberley. Everybody laughed.

Then Lavina sniffed.

"The gingerbread!" she said. "It's done."

She dug the Dutch oven out of the coals, and when she lifted off the ashy iron lid, a delicious fragrance escaped into the air, like one of the pent-up genies in the *Arabian Nights*. Lavina cut it into thirteen equal pieces, and they all ate gingerbread together, down to the last crumb, sitting around the friendly campfire on the evening of the great San Francisco earthquake.

CHAPTER TWENTY-ONE
The Cumming Family Motto

"The last composition of the year is free," Miss Hazlem said. "You may choose your own topics."

"Anything at all?" groaned the class. "Too hard!"

Lavina was not listening. She made her pen fly across the blank paper, scattering blots behind it. Meanwhile, Miss Hazlem wrote suggestions on the blackboard:

Who am I?
My Dreams
A Journey
When I Grow Up . . .
I Will Always Remember . . .

Lavina called her composition "Courage." She wrote: "My family has a motto that came over from Scotland with them. It is a single word: 'Courage.'"

A motto is a special saying that you paint on

your shield if you are a knight. When my father sent me to California, he wrote my name and address on a card and pinned it to my dress. I am not a knight. I am Lavina Cumming. So I must wear the Cumming family motto inside of me.

She paused and chewed her pen. "What is courage?" she wrote, rather grandly she thought. The answer was not so easy. She chewed the pen for several minutes before she went on. "Courage helps you do what you don't want to do, but must, and it helps you fight."

Lavina leaned her cheek upon her fist and stared at the paper without seeing it. Instead she saw huge walls of rock, silent canyons, cactus thorns. She heard bullets scream past her ears.

"Courage makes you brave," she wrote.

She felt the whole world buck like a wild horse. She saw the ocean eat the buildings along the edge of the bay.

"Many people showed courage during the earthquake," she continued. "A bed fell on my Aunt Agnes, and her house was wrecked, but she went right on."

The Cerro Prieto rose before Lavina's mind's eye. She saw herself standing halfway up the dark hill, with Chummy's reins in her hand.

Once I wanted to climb a mountain near my home in Arizona, but it was so hard that several times I quit and came home bleeding. Finally I did it. I stood on the top. La Cima is the name of that place, the summit, and I call the country all around my home Lavinalandia. Sometimes it takes courage to have hope and try again.

Lavina glanced around the classroom, where many pens were now at work. From the desk in front of her, she heard Susan sigh heavily. Birdie dipped her pen neatly in her inkwell; Miss Hazlem corrected papers at her own desk; in the sunny window the goldfish glittered in the bowl.

"Sometimes," wrote Lavina, "I believe courage is in my head, and sometimes in my heart." For an instant her thoughts slipped into Spanish, where "heart" was *corazón*, and one way to say "courage" was *coraje*. But *coraje* also meant "anger."

"Sometimes anger makes you brave," she wrote.

I think courage comes from the same place as anger, fear, and hope. It's deep inside. It's the core. I guess love comes from that place, too, so maybe the best word for it, after all, is heart.

I hope that I can go home again someday.

The next day Miss Hazlem asked Lavina to stay after school, but she asked with a smile, so Lavina knew that she wasn't in trouble. Puzzled, Lavina made a neat pile of her books and sat still while the other children filed out of the room.

"We'll wait," whispered Susan as she went by.

"Come here, Lavina." Miss Hazlem patted the chair beside her desk. "This composition is good."

Lavina saw a high mark at the top, and she felt her cheeks burn. "Thank you."

Up so close, Lavina could see the individual hairs, just like anyone else's, in Miss Hazlem's polished mahogany braids, and she could even hear the tiny ticking of the gold watch pinned to her teacher's starched white shirtwaist. Its hands pointed to five minutes past four o'clock.

"How does she keep her shirtwaist crisp all day?" thought Lavina. Her own middy blouse was limp by noon.

"Lavina, I believe you could do seventh-grade work next year," said Miss Hazlem. "You might skip a grade. What would you say to that?"

"Oh, no!"

"Why, what's the matter?"

"And leave my friends?"

"They would still be your friends," said Miss Hazlem.

Lavina gazed down at her paper and made no answer. Miss Hazlem's suggestion took her breath away.

"You will be here next year, won't you?"

At this Lavina looked up. "I think so," she said slowly.

"Will you go home for a visit this summer?"

"I don't know yet."

Miss Hazlem quickly changed the subject. "I like this part about 'La Cima,'" she said, tapping Lavina's composition with a manicured fingernail. "Is that a real mountain?"

"Oh, yes," said Lavina. "It's all true."

I Am Lavina Cumming

"And you speak Spanish?"

"Yes. We all do, except Father."

"A beautiful language," said Miss Hazlem. "You are very lucky."

"Me?"

"Yes, indeed. Languages are like countries. The more you know, the more you understand about the world."

"Miss Hazlem, how did you get to be a teacher?"

"Ah!" She gave Lavina a searching look with her warm brown eyes. "Well, first I graduated from high school. In a few years, I'm sure you will, too. Then I went to teachers' college, and then I passed an examination and received a teaching certificate."

"I see." Lavina rose, clutching her book and her composition to her chest. "Thank you."

"One step at a time," said Miss Hazlem kindly, rising also.

"What did she want?" asked Birdie.

"She returned my composition, that's all."

Lavina did not want to talk about skipping a grade; perhaps it would never happen, after all. She stuffed "Courage" into her arithmetic book, and the three girls set off down Vine Street together.

"I'll bet you wrote the best composition in the class."

"And I'll bet you speak the best piece, Susan. And Birdie has the prettiest handwriting. She never makes an ink blot."

Birdie showed her dimples; her cap of hair was perfectly neat, as always. "I really don't care about being the best at anything," she said comfortably.

"The program is *tomorrow*," said Susan. "Let's practice our pieces one more time."

Lavina drew a deep breath, and to the rhythm of their footsteps on the sidewalk, she began.

"My heart leaps up when I behold—"

I Am Lavina Cumming

CHAPTER TWENTY-TWO
Home, Sweet Home

"What's in your suitcase, Lavina?" said Bridget. "Sure, it weighs a ton."

Among her clothes Lavina had tucked six large California oranges, each wrapped in a square of green tissue paper, as homecoming presents for Father and her brothers. But she did not admit this, even to Bridget.

Bridget rested for a moment beside the marble lady on the second-floor landing. After the earthquake, Cousin Maude had spent days gluing the statue together again, and Lavina still marveled at her success. You could hardly detect the hairline cracks in the lady's small cool smile. And Faith, Hope, Charity, and Love all hung in their old places again, newly framed.

"The cab is here, Lavina," called Cousin Maude from the bottom of the stairs.

Lavina gave her and Aggie each a dutiful kiss.

"I'm sorry you'll miss the wedding," said Cousin Maude.

For Cousin Maude was going to marry Mr. Moberley. This news was a surprise, and yet not a surprise.

"Aggie and Freddy will make such a lovely flower girl and page boy," Cousin Maude continued. Lavina felt a bubble of laughter grow larger and larger inside her until she thought she would pop.

"Freddy says he won't do it," said Aggie.

Cousin Maude only smiled.

"And neither of us is *ever* taking another piano lesson."

"We'll see about that," said her mother.

In some ways the old Aggie was back, but in other ways she had changed. She was politer to Lavina, and because she was rather afraid of Freddy, she watched her step when he visited. Meanwhile Cousin Maude floated around the house in a radiant mood, not paying much attention to Aggie's whims. The ear trumpet did not reappear after the earthquake.

In the street Bridget gave Lavina a squeeze that left her gasping.

"Be off with you now." Bridget released her.

Lavina picked up her traveling basket, which she had dropped. "What will you do, Bridget?"

"Sure and I'll stay right here. I'd rather not get married till I save myself a good nest egg, and so I told the gentleman himself. If he wants to wait, he can."

"Will he?"

Bridget only laughed.

The cab driver helped Aunt Agnes into the buggy,

for she planned to accompany Lavina as far as Watsonville. As they rattled away, Lavina leaned out the window and threw a kiss backward toward 19 Vine Street.

Side by side, Aunt Agnes and Lavina waited in the Watsonville depot for Lavina's train.

"I really hate to send you alone, dear," fretted Aunt Agnes, "but I can see no other way. I can't go. Maudie can't go."

"I'm not afraid," said Lavina. "I've done it before."

"We'd better pin some sort of message on your dress," said the old lady, "in case of trouble."

Politely but firmly, Lavina said, "No, thank you, Aunt Agnes. If I need help, I can tell people, 'I am Lavina Cumming, from the Bosque Ranch near Calabasas, Arizona Territory, and I am going home.'"

Aunt Agnes threw up her hands with a laugh. "Very well. But Lavina, I do want you to come back."

Lavina looked down at her shiny new button boots, the first she had ever owned, and a full size larger than the shoes she had worn last September.

"I know that you've been homesick," Aunt Agnes went on, "and I'm sorry about our little misunderstandings."

"I'm sorry, too," mumbled Lavina in embarrassment. Why didn't grown-ups ever know when to stop talking?

"Confession is good for the soul, Lavina, but hard on the reputation."

Lavina looked up. What did she mean?

"A bad temper is my besetting sin, my dear," said her aunt. "A lady should always control her temper, and I've been trying for seventy years without success."

She sighed. "But I keep trying."

Lavina was amazed. Aunt Agnes still trying to improve herself? Aunt Agnes not a lady?

"It's hard—"

"Yes, child?"

"It's hard to be a lady!"

"Yes. It has nothing to do with what's on the outside, you know. It's not a matter of education, or money. A lady is kind, courteous, and considerate of others."

Why, she sounded exactly like Father, Lavina thought.

"Anger can cause great damage. Do you know why I am telling you this, child?"

Lavina shook her head.

"Because you remind me of someone."

"Father?"

Aunt Agnes shook her head. "No, a girl I once knew, long, long ago. Her name was Agnes."

"Oh!" said Lavina and felt herself blushing.

They sat in silence for a moment.

"This marriage is a good thing," said Aunt Agnes. She seemed to be thinking out loud. "For Maudie, and for Aggie, too . . . she's been so terribly spoiled and lonesome. Of course I always tried not to interfere." Here a little uncertainty crept into Aunt Agnes's tone, as though she did not quite believe her own words.

I Am Lavina Cumming

Snip! Snip! Lavina remembered Aggie's tangled blond ringlets falling to the ground, and suddenly she realized how much Aunt Agnes had enjoyed herself that day.

"Having you was good for Aggie, but Freddy—" and now Aunt Agnes gave a deep, surprising chuckle, "Freddy will be even better."

"They'll fight like cats and dogs," thought Lavina. "But tomorrow I'll be home."

She would see her own brothers and Father and Luz and the dogs and the horses. She would smell mesquite smoke, and taste Luz's tortillas and beans, and feel strong sunlight on her hair. Soon, soon she would saddle Chummy and ride through the hills with John again.

Aunt Agnes was not finished yet. "Of course I'm alone now, but it's not just for your company that I want you to come back," she said. "It's for your own sake, too."

On the last day of school, Miss Hazlem had presented Lavina with a beautiful prize book illustrated with colored pictures. It was called *Lamb's Tales from Shakespeare*. Now it lay inside Lavina's traveling basket, along with Princess Perizade, a box of caramels from Susan and Birdie, and her latest letter from Father.

"You should go to high school, Lavina, and you can't do that on the ranch, can you?"

"No," said Lavina. "There isn't one."

She decided to tell her great new idea to Aunt Agnes.

"I'm going to be a schoolteacher, Aunt Agnes. So I

must go to high school *and* teachers' college. And then—" Lavina gave a bounce in her seat, and her pigtails swung from side to side. "Then I'll teach school in Arizona and make my own money and have my very own automobile!"

"Mercy!" said Aunt Agnes. "You *have* been thinking ahead. But perhaps someday you'll marry and have a family?"

"Maybe," said Lavina.

That was Birdie's dream, while Susan said actresses should never marry.

"I want to stand on my own two feet," Lavina thought.

She couldn't quite imagine a family, but an automobile was easy. What fun to drive it herself at amazing speeds up to twenty-five miles an hour, just like the president's dashing daughter, Miss Alice Roosevelt!

"And I want my own ranch someday, too," she thought.

"You must come back, dear. Your father agrees with me. Things will be different, of course. You have two homes now," said Aunt Agnes decisively.

She fumbled through the contents of her handbag. A crystal bottle of smelling salts. A lace-edged handkerchief. A coin purse. A fan. And finally a railroad ticket and a small red velvet pouch.

"Your father bought your ticket home," said Aunt Agnes, "but I have bought your return ticket. Here. No, no, don't interrupt. It's rude. I am still talking."

She held out the little velvet bag.

"This was mine, and now it's yours. Well, well.

Enough said. Go ahead, open it, child."

"Oh!"

A tiny gold locket and chain spilled into Lavina's palm. The locket was heart shaped and perfectly plain and smooth except for one small, sharp dent near the point of the heart. Lavina touched it inquiringly with her fingertip.

"That is a tooth mark," said Aunt Agnes, drawing herself up with great dignity, but also with a twinkle in her eye. "Once, when I was about your age, I regret to say I bit it."

Lavina threw her arms around the old lady, crutch and all. Then they heard the whistle of Lavina's train.

"Good-bye, my dear child," said Aunt Agnes. She removed her spectacles and wiped them. "Now, remember—"

"Don't get off the train!" said Lavina. "Good-bye, Aunt Agnes. Thank you, thank you, thank you."

Aunt Agnes's white handkerchief waved and waved, shrank to a speck, and disappeared in a cloud of steam.

Late on the following afternoon, a tired and grubby but very happy Lavina leaned out the window of the burro train as it made its lazy way along Sonoita Creek. The Arizona sky was as splendid as ever; you could almost drink it, she thought. However, she had to admit that the burro was slow. Princess Perizade smiled sweetly at the sign that warned passengers, "DO NOT SPIT," but Lavina was impatient. She had read her new book from cover to cover and had reread Father's letter several times.

"I hear excellent reports of you, Daughtie," he wrote. "Your Aunt Agnes says that she has invited you to live with her until you finish your education."

"Ordered me is more like it," thought Lavina, fingering the little locket that hung around her neck. She still wanted to go home, but she no longer felt like a captive.

Father's beautiful script continued: "As long as we can afford the train tickets, you will spend your summers on the Bosque Ranch, for I miss my favorite daughter. The boys and I will meet you in Squashville when your train comes in."

"I'll tell them about the earthquake," Lavina said to herself. "Why, I have my own stories now."

She felt like a heroine rolling in triumph across Arizona. She leaned her chin on her folded hands, and for many miles she watched for a certain landmark. Then at last she saw it, standing pale blue at a great distance: San Cayetano Peak, with the Bosque Ranch at its western foot.

Lavinalandia.

"My heart leaps up," she said aloud. "Oh, my heart leaps up!"

Afterword

My father's mother, Lavina Cumming Lowell, was born in Arizona Territory one hundred years ago. She lived on a ranch there until she was ten, when her father sent her to California to be educated. This book is based on stories she told about her western girlhood. The tale of her first trip to California, all alone on the train, was probably the one she told most often.

In our family, storytelling happened all the time: in Grandmama's ranch house kitchen, in the car crossing the desert at sixty miles an hour, over the turkey bones on Christmas Day, at bedtime after a long summer day, and always around campfires.

My grandmother began by asking her grandchildren: "Would you like to hear a *true* story?"

And, rather reluctantly, we would say, "Yes, a true story," for we knew that was the answer Grandmama wanted to hear. Her stories were unforgettable and a great gift to us—yet sometimes we did yearn for fantasy!

As I wrote this book, I imagined the parts of her life that I did not know, and I changed some details, but I also came to understand that true stories and imaginary stories are not so different after all. Given that choice, I would still answer, "Yes, a true story," because I believe that every good story, in its own way, is true.

—Susan Lowell
Tucson, Arizona
January 1993

SUSAN LOWELL is the author of four books for adults and eight for children, including *The Three Little Javelinas*. She was born in Chihuahua, Mexico, and is a fourth-generation Arizonan, descended from a long line of prospectors, explorers, ranchers, farmers, and school-marms. She and her husband and their two daughters divide their time between Tucson and a ranch near the Mexican border.

I Am Lavina Cumming was named the Children's Book of the Year in 1994 by the Mountains and Plains Booksellers' Association.

Milkweed Editions

Founded in 1979, Milkweed Editions is the largest independent, nonprofit literary publisher in the United States. Milkweed publishes with the intention of making a humane impact on society, in the belief that good writing can transform the human heart and spirit. Within this mission, Milkweed publishes in five areas: fiction, nonfiction, poetry, children's literature for middle-grade readers, and the World As Home—books about our relationship with the natural world.

Join Us

Milkweed depends on the generosity of foundations and individuals like you, in addition to the sales of its books. In an increasingly consolidated and bottom-line-driven publishing world, your support allows us to select and publish books on the basis of their literary quality and the depth of their message. Please visit our Web site (www.milkweed.org) or contact us at (800) 520-6455 to learn more about our donor program.

The $66 Summer
John Armistead

MILKWEED PRIZE FOR CHILDREN'S LITERATURE
NEW YORK PUBLIC LIBRARY BEST BOOKS OF THE YEAR:
"BOOKS FOR THE TEEN AGE"

A story of interracial friendships in the segregation-era South.

The Return of Gabriel
John Armistead

A story of Freedom Summer.

The Ocean Within
V. M. Caldwell

MILKWEED PRIZE FOR CHILDREN'S LITERATURE

Focuses on an older child adopted into a large,
extended family.

Tides
V. M. Caldwell

The sequel to *The Ocean Within,* this book deals with
the troubles of older siblings.

Alligator Crossing
Marjory Stoneman Douglas

Features the wildlife of the Everglades just before it was declared a national park.

Perfect
Natasha Friend

MILKWEED PRIZE FOR CHILDREN'S LITERATURE

A thirteen-year-old girl struggles with bulimia after her father dies.

Parents Wanted
George Harrar

MILKWEED PRIZE FOR CHILDREN'S LITERATURE

Focuses on the adoption of a boy with ADD

The Trouble with Jeremy Chance
George Harrar

BANK STREET COLLEGE BEST CHILDREN'S BOOKS OF THE YEAR

Father-son conflict during the final days of World War I.

No Place
Kay Haugaard

Based on a true story of Latino youth who create an inner-city park.

The Monkey Thief
Aileen Kilgore Henderson

NEW YORK PUBLIC LIBRARY BEST BOOKS OF THE YEAR: "BOOKS FOR THE TEEN AGE"

A twelve-year-old boy is sent to live with his uncle in a Costa Rican rain forest.

Hard Times for Jake Smith
Aileen Kilgore Henderson

A girl searches for her family in the Depression-era South.

The Summer of the Bonepile Monster
Aileen Kilgore Henderson

MILKWEED PRIZE FOR CHILDREN'S LITERATURE

A brother and sister spend the summer with their great-grandmother in the South.

Treasure of Panther Peak
Aileen Kilgore Henderson

NEW YORK PUBLIC LIBRARY BEST BOOKS OF THE YEAR: "BOOKS FOR THE TEEN AGE"

A twelve-year-old girl adjusts to her new life in Big Bend National Park.

The Boy with Paper Wings
Susan Lowell

This story about a feverish boy's imagined battles includes paper-folding instructions.

The Secret of the Ruby Ring
Yvonne MacGrory

A blend of time travel and historical fiction set in 1885 Ireland.

Emma and the Ruby Ring
Yvonne MacGrory

A tale of time travel to nineteenth-century Ireland.

A Bride for Anna's Papa
Isabel R. Marvin

MILKWEED PRIZE FOR CHILDREN'S LITERATURE

Life on Minnesota's Iron Range in the early 1900s.

Minnie
Annie M. G. Schmidt

A cat turns into a woman and helps a hapless newspaperman.

A Small Boat at the Bottom of the Sea
John Thomson

Donovan's summer with his ailing aunt and mysterious uncle on the Puget Sound tests his convictions.

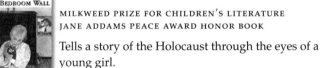

The Dog with Golden Eyes
Frances Wilbur

MILKWEED PRIZE FOR CHILDREN'S LITERATURE

A young girl's dream of owning a dog comes true, but it may be more than she's bargained for.

Behind the Bedroom Wall
Laura E. Williams

MILKWEED PRIZE FOR CHILDREN'S LITERATURE
JANE ADDAMS PEACE AWARD HONOR BOOK

Tells a story of the Holocaust through the eyes of a young girl.

The Spider's Web
Laura E. Williams

A young girl in a neo-Nazi group sets off a chain of events when she's befriended by an old German woman.

Printed on acid-free 50# Fraser Trade book paper
by Friesen Corporation.